# WHAT IT TAKES TO BE THE MAN

WHAT IT TAKES TO BE THE MAN

# CLR JR.

*Story by*

***Charles Lee Robinson Jr.***

# WHAT IT TAKES TO BE THE MAN

Copyright © 2025 Charles Lee Robinson Jr. All rights reserved.

No part of this book may be reproduced or transmitted in any form or by any means, graphic, electronic, or mechanical, including photocopying, recording, taping, or by any information storage retrieval without the permission, in writing, of the publisher. For more information, send an email to charlesleerobinsonjr@gmail.com

Casual Comfort Publication, LLC

USA / Florida

My website: amazon.com/author/robinsonc

# WHAT IT TAKES TO BE THE MAN

**Dedicated to the men who have gone through a struggle**

**Black Men deserve respect because we have to work twice as hard!**

*Psalms 34:18*

*The LORD is close to the brokenhearted and saves those who are crushed in spirit.*

# WHAT IT TAKES TO BE THE MAN

Men go through *struggles* like animals in the winter.

They search for survival, and they only rely on their instincts.

    Pleasure, sometimes, is their escape, searching for

*Love* with a rope around their throat.

He has no vision, and he won't listen

Until his life comes crashing *down.*

    *****From Charles Lee Robinson Jr.*

Your choices in life help mold your future.

    *****PEN NAME: CLR JR.

WHAT IT TAKES TO BE THE MAN

# THE TABLE OF CONTENTS

PROLOGUE - |

Chapter 1 – Incest Desires |

Chapter 2 – The Family Business |

Chapter 3 – You Can't Trust Family |

Chapter 4 – Embracing Manhood |

Chapter 5 – Dating A Married Woman |

Chapter 6 – Going Backwards |

Chapter 7 – Dealing With A Nightmare |

Chapter 8 – The Beginning Of Change |

Chapter 9 – A Heavy Load To Bear |

Chapter 10 – Trusting My Decision |

Chapter 11 – A Product of Your Environment |

Chapter 12 – Lost All Respect |

Chapter 13 – Let Downs And Rejections |

Chapter 14 – A Decisive Conclusion |

Chapter 15 – Maneuvering Through Life |

WHAT IT TAKES TO BE THE MAN

# THE TABLE OF CONTENTS

Chapter 16 – Stress is Building |

Chapter 17 – Disloyal and Betrayed |

Chapter 18 – Trying To Find My Way |

Chapter 19 – Taking What Life Throws At You |

Chapter 20 – Make It All Make Sense |

Chapter 21 – Lining With The Stars |

Chapter 22 – Escaped Unscathed |

Chapter 23 – Deceit Unveiled |

Chapter 24 – A Dual Reflection |

Chapter 25 – Disloyal And Betrayed |

Chapter 26 – From Defeat To Triumph |

-

# WHAT IT TAKES TO BE THE MAN

### *A Black Man's Prayer*

*Dear Father God, my days are not easy; my walk in life isn't guaranteed, so I pray that you make my journey uncomplicated. Although, in life, you said there would be good days and bad, I hope that you make my walk diligent and my choices resilient. I understand you give the most challenging jobs to your soldiers, and I am willing to take on all obstacles and distractions as long as you walk with me. I want to Thank you, Lord, in Jesus' name. Amen!*

WHAT IT TAKES TO BE THE MAN

# PROLOGUE

They say a man should get a woman like his Momma, but I am unsure. Now, don't get me wrong—I love my Momma. Any man who doesn't is the problem.

But, in my story, I have to give up the straight facts. They say women don't cheat or rarely cheat, but I must say, that's a lie. I am not saying all women do, but some wander off into another man's arms, or should I say bed, for no apparent reason.

I say all that to say is, I saw my Momma cheat on my Dad with a man I had never seen before. You may say I am crazy, or maybe I was seeing and hearing things, but I wasn't.

I wanted to beat that man's ass for making my Momma scream like that. What was he doing to her? Later on in life, I found out that he was fucking the shit out of my Momma.

I didn't tell Dad like a good little boy, but maybe I should have. I am DeVon Edwin Bell, and the story started like this: I was nearing the age to go to kindergarten. That's an age you wouldn't think a young boy would remember anything, right? Wrong. Even up in age, I have never forgotten about it. I wonder why.

# WHAT IT TAKES TO BE THE MAN

My parents were up early, having their morning coffee, and Dad was preparing his lunch for work. I was also up early and sat at the kitchen table with them.

"I hope you have a good day at work, it's payday, so you better bring your ass right home?" Momma said.

"What, I am, after I get me a drink," Dad chuckled.

"I am not playing with you, we have bills to pay, that fucking alcohol can wait."

"I am grown, you don't tell me what to do,"

"You keep thinking that, I am not playing with you, the light bill needs to be paid today, or they are shutting the lights off,"

"I said, I will be here when I get off. I am going to pay the light bill, don't boss me around," Dad said as he sipped his coffee and left the house.

My Momma looked at me and said, "Don't be stupid like your Dad." I was puzzled because, at that age, I didn't understand what was going on with the two of them. They argued and fought a lot. I mean, I would see Momma in Dad's face all the time, hitting and cursing at him. He would always try to protect his face. It made me upset at night, but what could I do? I was just a little boy.

# WHAT IT TAKES TO BE THE MAN

After Dad left for work, Momma sent me upstairs to my room. I heard her get into the shower. She was singing a Black Butterfly song. She had a great voice.

I lay down on my bed and acted like I was sleeping. I wasn't tired; I was being a nosy little boy. I heard Momma walk by my room to see if I was asleep, so I lay still and closed my eyes tightly.

When I heard the doorbell ring, I got up and tiptoed to see who it was. Momma was in a robe, so maybe it was family. Damn, was I so wrong?

The door opened, and Momma was cheerful, and so was this man with long curly hair and a light complexion. I hid behind the door, and my heart started beating. Momma smiled and so did he.

She let him come in and said, "Let me make sure that my son is still sleeping." In a light whisper, the man said, "Okay." I tiptoed back into my bed, pulled the covers up my cheekbone, and turned on my side so she couldn't see my face.

Minutes later, Momma said," "Come on up, my son is sleeping, but don't make a noise." "All right," He said in a whisper.

I heard them pass my room and head to Momma and Dad's. As soon as the door closed, I got up, stuck my head out of my door, and just listened.

## WHAT IT TAKES TO BE THE MAN

*"Oh, ah, boy, you are giving it to me real good, oh Jesus, oh, give it to me. "Take it, take all of it, ah, ooh, oh, whoa. He said. "Yes, make me cum, make it cum,"*

Those sounds and words were heard for at least thirty minutes, and then I heard slapping. I thought the man was beating on my Momma, so I went to the door and looked through the keyhole. What I saw may have ruined me for life.

That man was behind my Momma with his naked-yellow ass, and he was striking her. She was stuttering, praying, and grabbing for the thin air. I started crying, and I think they heard me because the noise stopped after I heard Momma and that man say, "Oh, I am cummin, I am cummin, oh shit, this is so good," "Oh yeah, ah, ah, I am cumin, damn, damn, that pussy is good,"

I jumped into my bed and put the covers over my head. I heard them scuffling around to get dressed, but I shut my eyes tightly. Momma's door opened, and I heard her trying to rush the man out. I think she called him Luis. As they were heading towards the door, my nosy ass jumped up to watch Momma walk him out. They kissed, and he left. Momma turned around, and I stared at her as I watched.

"What in the hell are you doing up?" I didn't say a word. "What did you see, what did you see, what did you hear," Momma asked as she grabbed my shirt by the neck and shook me violently.

## WHAT IT TAKES TO BE THE MAN

"Nothing, Momma, nothing," I whispered in fear. "You had better not say anything to anyone, not even you, Dad, because if you do, I am going to whip your little ass good. Do you hear me?"

I could tell Momma was serious, and I didn't want that belt or a tree branch beating my ass. I went back to bed, and I acted as if the shit never happened. But I remembered, but I don't think Momma thought I did.

That was the beginning of me seeing the world and even my Momma in a different light. Dad never found out, but those noises, the moans and groans, made me sick to my stomach every time I thought about them. This experience altered the beginning of my life, but what came next was even worse than that.

# Chapter

# 1

## *Incest Desires*

I never saw that Luis guy at our house, but once I started going to school, I saw him in the neighborhood, either walking or riding a bike. I acted like I didn't see him and kept walking. I believe he knew who I was, however. I wasn't sure, but it was just a hunch.

The following year, I started school, which led Momma to get a job. She and Dad couldn't agree on the responsibilities in the house. I am not sure, but the way my Momma saw it, the man was supposed to be the head of the household. That was a lesson learned.

Since my parents were working, they had to find me a babysitter. The babysitters were expensive, so Momma had a great idea; she let her little sister, my Aunt Ella, babysit me.

# WHAT IT TAKES TO BE THE MAN

They thought it would be grand and even sought to pay her. Ella and I always had a good relationship. Although she was ten years older than me, she was always nice when I saw her.

Momma and Daddy's idea wasn't as great as they thought it would be; at least not for me, it wasn't. As the months passed, I noticed something different about Ella; she became more playful with me. I never knew that deep down, she wanted to fuck a little boy.

It all started as a game. But, damn, did it change one afternoon. I got out of kindergarten for half a day, my parents wouldn't be home until the evening, and that's when her sexual advances towards me went into full motion. What could I do? I was just a kid. She started grinding on my pants. My dick would get hard, and I didn't understand what was going on with my body.

Daily, she would grope me, and eventually, she took me to bed. She would always make me promise not to tell Momma or anyone because she feared Momma would kill her. I stayed silent like a good little boy. Momma's ass-whooping's were legendary. I didn't want any part of that. Plus, I didn't know what she was doing to me was wrong.

Let's say she made me do everything, from licking and sucking on all of her body parts. Some of her body fluids had a funny taste and were very wet. At that age, I didn't know what cum was, but I know now.

# WHAT IT TAKES TO BE THE MAN

She would suck and lick on my dick. The sensation used to drive me up the wall. I always had to stop her because it seemed like I had to pee, but I guess that was the time that a man was supposed to cum. I realize that now. Momma started noticing something different about me because my dick started getting hard for no reason. At first, she and Dad thought it was a part of a boy growing up, but it got more noticeable, so Momma took me to the doctor.

The doctor couldn't explain it any more than Momma could. He said it was normal for a boy to have an erection. I kept my mouth closed. I didn't know my erection was stemming from her molesting me. I mean, how could I know?

Occasionally, Momma would take me back to the doctor, but the results were always the same. After a couple of years, things got a little more intense. Aunt Ella would invite her female friends to the house while my parents worked.

She and her friends would take turns rubbing and grabbing at my dick. I heard them say it was pretty big for a little boy. I didn't know how to keep them off me. I would run and hide, but I couldn't always get away. I will let you imagine the rest.

I guess Ella wanted to explore different things with me, and that's when she introduced me to anal sex. She wanted me to put my duck in her big ass. I was scared because I knew that shit comes out there, but she made me do it after she put something wet and slippery up there.

## WHAT IT TAKES TO BE THE MAN

She started grinding on my dick, but my body couldn't take it. I got this peeing sensation quickly, so I ran into the bathroom. She came behind me and asked me what was wrong. I told her I didn't know. It just seemed like I had to pee badly. But as time passed, that sensation took longer and longer to get to.

I believe my body got used to it. The molestation went on for about four years. Ella started touching me and molesting me when I was five. About the time I turned nine, her sex advances slowed down.

She figured I was getting older, and my chances of telling on her were more likely. I still didn't know what we were doing was wrong, but over time, when she slowed down and eventually stopped, I knew.

My body started feeling weird without the sex. After four years, I was used to it. I could tell my dick got bigger and longer. I guess, It was big for a young boy my age.

After that, I would wet my bed. Over a particular time, as I got older, I started having real wet dreams, and white stuff came out of me. I used to dream about sex with Ella because I didn't know better.

Ella was older and would stare at me when we had a family get-together, but she acted like she never touched me. I guess at that time, she was only having incest desires.

## WHAT IT TAKES TO BE THE MAN

It still sticks with me today. I know that Aunt Ella molested me, but I never told a soul up until this point because Momma would have killed her. She was lucky, but soon, I would be the unlucky one.

# Chapter 2

## *The Family Business*

At a young age, my body went through withdrawals, and there wasn't a dam thing I could do about it. I didn't understand it, and my Dad would never have those Dad to son conversations about sex, so I had to deal with the shit the best way I could.

Getting back into being a regular boy playing sports and having friends helped me break free a little bit, but every time I saw Ella, I started having flashbacks. I would go to the bathroom and stroke my dick and marvel at how big it was. I used to say to myself, if I have sex with a girl, I am going to kill her because it looked so big in my hands, but what in the hell did I know?

After a while, I got in control, and that's right, about the time I found out about our family business. Every weekend, we would get together over my Momma's second youngest sister, Tameeka. She was also my Aunt, but she was nothing like Ella. She was strict, intelligent, and she treated me like her son. I am not sure she knew that my Uncles, Keith and Darwin, Aunt Ella, my cousin Donia, her boyfriend Fred, and their friends were getting drugs together in her basement.

They got together every weekend to bag up some weed and some pills. They would smoke around me and even make me smoke and choke off that strong shit. I wondered why they always tried to make me high. Blowing all that smoke on a kid's face could make you sick or addicted at a young age.

I would turn it down most of the time, but sometimes, they would grab me and give me a shotgun, meaning blowing all that marijuana smoke down my nostrils. That shit made me choke, and my eyes water. Why were they trying to get me to do this? Was smoking weed part of a boy growing up and doing grown-up things?

It was always the same thing: they would say, don't tell your Momma because she would kill us. Was my Momma a killer? Why did they keep saying that? It left me confused as a little boy.

After time went by, I guess you can say the family business was getting bigger because more people started coming, and more of these enormous garbage bags would be delivered. Ten to twenty large bags full of weed and pills—they called the pills Black Beauty.

# WHAT IT TAKES TO BE THE MAN

There were never any money shortages. The money flowed in until my cousins Donia and Fred decided to break away from the rest of the family and start their business.

They took most of the customers, so suddenly, everyone else started going their separate ways. Donia and Fred began having children, and their business became more significant.

They got run down by the FBI, and their business shut down instantly. They both went to jail, and their children were taken. Momma tried to get the children from the foster home, but six children would be difficult to take care of. The judge wanted to split up Donia's children. Momma couldn't get them. They ended up separated at different foster homes.

At the time, I didn't know that selling drugs was illegal. No one ever told me that. I was just young and just watching grown-ups do grown-up shit.

Shortly after, My uncle ended up in jail for a lengthy time, and everything ceased altogether. Watching this as a young boy, I knew I didn't want to follow in the footsteps of my family members. They were starting to end up on the drugs they sold and in jail. I barely saw them after that. It was years and years before everyone started emerging again. By that time, I was in my late teens. Times have changed over the years, and so has my mind.

# Chapter 3

## *You can't trust family*

As I got into my late teens, my Aunt Ella got herself a boyfriend named Carlton. Carlton was a nice guy, laid-back, and loved to joke. They were supposed to get Married in my Momma's house. He was set to go to the Marines, and she would leave the country to meet him.

The wedding happened later that year, and my Momma made all the other ladies' clothes. It was a small but really nice wedding. No more than a year later, Ella left the country to meet him. She was delighted when she got on that plane and we dropped her off.

We watched the planned take-off, and while everybody was happy, I kept thinking about what she had done to me as a little boy. I sure hope God has something for her.

# WHAT IT TAKES TO BE THE MAN

During that time, it seemed like all of my older family members were locked up in jail or dead. That was when I decided to drop out of school in the 11th grade. I was so damn stupid.

I guess because I followed most of my cousins. They wanted a glamorous life. They loved to be like the drug dealers in our neighborhood. While they were selling drugs, I started looking for a job.

I already knew where that life could lead you. My cousins gambled a lot. They loved shooting dice. One time, while we were at a dice game, a guy named Danny Prescot shot my cousin Tony Bell and killed him. I promised never to play dice again.

My cousins were robbing people, but I found a job, and I worked. I thought I would never do what they did, but never say never. I got fired from my job for speaking up for myself. Caucasians don't like that. I was never taught about racism, but I had to learn the hard way.

I lost several jobs because I thought I could plead my case as a man, but I sadly found out it was only for a specific type of man. So being backed into a corner will make a man do strange shit to pay those bills.

I suddenly realized that I had to sell drugs, too. My cousins loved living the fast life, but I was always thinking about saving my money so I could get away from that illegal shit; plus, I never stopped looking for another job.

One night, while we were selling out of a house, some guys tried to rob us. My cousin, Big Henny, was almost sliced with a knife. We went toe to toe with those robbers. They ran like the bitches they were after we were done with them.

That's when I realized how dangerous this street shit was. I was so happy when I found another job. I worked at a restaurant where I met this pretty girl named Regina Allen. I heard she had a crush on me.

Regina and I became very close on the job. I like her because she constantly flirted and made me laugh. All that sex talk on the job drove me crazy. I haven't had sex since I was molested. I was nervous. She kept saying that she wanted me to sleep with her. She said that her pussy would drown me. What the hell was she talking about? I was still green until then, wet behind the ears.

I would tell my cousins about her, and they would tell me to fuck her hard. I wasn't sure what that meant, but I soon found out when I saw my cousins bring girls into my cousin Harold's house.

Girls came in and out of that house. You could hear girls screaming while they were cummin in every room. I think I had to learn fast because my cousins were sleeping with different girls daily.

## WHAT IT TAKES TO BE THE MAN

Since my cousin Harold knew I was working and not selling drugs like everyone else, he asked me to be a roommate and pay half the bills. I was ecstatic because Momma and Dad were tired of me, and they bothered me about getting my GED or returning to school.

They constantly said I needed to return to school for a better job. I thought they were just two parents getting on my damn nerves, but the more I saw how the world was, I started to think about it.

Anyway, I went half with Harold and had my room in the house. I started bringing Regina over, and we would chill. All my cousins thought she was a cool girl.

One night, Regina wanted to go into my room and have sex with me, so I took her with me to my room. We started kissing and touching each other. I noticed that my dick wasn't getting hard. I didn't understand it. She asked me what was wrong, but I didn't know and couldn't explain what was happening.

We tried over and over again with no luck. I was embarrassed and didn't know what to do. She thought it was okay that we tried another day.

Again, we tried, but no luck. What the fuck is wrong with me? My dick is long and big when it gets hard. It gets very hard when I dream and wake up in the morning. I was clueless.

## WHAT IT TAKES TO BE THE MAN

Finally, after weeks of trying, my dick got hard and big, and soon as I was about to insert it in her, that muthafucka went down. I was shocked. She asked me if I was okay; I said yes, but I felt like crying deep down.

We tried again, and it finally worked, but it only lasted two minutes, and I saw that white shit come out of my dick. My body started shaking, so I guess that was cum or an orgasm. I had heard about them by listening to my cousins talk about having sex with girls.

As time went on, the sex got better, at least I thought. One day, I had to work, and Regina didn't. When I got off, I went home. I was surprised to see Regina sitting at the house with all my male cousins while watching football.

Everyone, for some reason, looked strange in the face. They had smirks, and I didn't understand that. I asked her how long she had been waiting for me, and she said an hour. I thought nothing of it then, but it became a pattern over time, even when I told her not to show up at my house unless I was there.

It all went down one day when I called into work, and she was off. I didn't tell her I didn't work, so I went out for a while and came home.

None of my cousins were there. It was too damn quiet. The house is never this silent. I started to go to my bedroom, but I heard a woman's voice. I tiptoed to Harold's door, and I could hear him

# WHAT IT TAKES TO BE THE MAN

fucking the shit out of some girl. The voice sounded familiar. The moans and groans got louder. "Oh, you are giving it to me baby, oh, yes, tear it up, tear it up, oh my gosh, damm, damn," She yelled. *"You love this shit, don't you, take all of it, take it, "Grab my hair, grab my hair, and slap that big ass, Daddy," She said. "Take every inch, come here, and take it, don't run" "Oh, I am cummin, I'm cumin," "Yes, ah, take it all, oh, here it cums, I am cummin,"* They yelled loudly.

That voice sounded so familiar. I grabbed my dick and held it because Harold was fucking shit out of that girl. I got a little nosy, so I looked through the keyhole. I damn there blew a gasket; what the fuck. I knew that voice, and I was right. It was familiar. It was Regina.

Tears came down my eyes; He was fucking my girl; I couldn't believe it. I knew that I was having sex problems, but why would she fuck my first cousin? Why would my cousin do this shit to me? I didn't know this was a part of the game.

I couldn't take it anymore. I knocked that damn door down. Regina grabbed the sheets, and she was terrified. Harold tried to grab his underwear and clothes, but he couldn't because I was kicking his naked ass. "It was her fault. It was her, not me," He yelled.

"It was you; stop lying," She yelled.

# WHAT IT TAKES TO BE THE MAN

"Fuck this shit, and it was both of you, I am out of this bitch, you hear me Harold, and Regina, you are a slut, now get the fuck out, now,"

"You don't have to go anywhere," Harold said. Regina started to get up, but once he said that, she didn't; she just got back under the covers. "Okay, fuck you, I am going, and I am getting all my things," I yelled as I exited his room. I couldn't believe that slut stayed with him.

I was so hurt that I cried leaving that house. I felt devastated. What would drive her to do that to me? You can't even trust your family because they will take great pride in stabbing you in your back.

I quit my job that same day because I couldn't work with Regina; weeks later, I heard my cousin Harold dumped her ass for a better-looking girl. She looked foolish, my cousin Big Henny said.

Now, I know why they all had smiles, and who knows who else she slept with? Why my cousins couldn't tell me she was sleeping with Harold? I know we are all family, but damn, you're going to have me look foolish like that?

I promised never to put myself in that situation again. I will not bring any woman around them because I can't trust them. I know she was just as wrong for doing what she did, but I am not taking any chances. The lessons learned came far in between.

# Chapter

# 4

## *Embracing Manhood*

I often made terrible decisions while trying to find myself as a man. I stopped hanging out with my cousins and started being around the guys I grew up with. And, of course, they sold drugs, too, but some of them were into girls, too.

At the time, my Momma said that Ella had three children with her new husband and that they would be back in the USA for a short period. I was older, and my resentment had gone away. I couldn't wait to see her family.

I was a young man, and it was my time to find a woman I could call mine. Women played games, and I constantly caught them cheating on me. The bullshit went on for a while until I met Yvonne Stapleton. She was nice at first, but somehow, that continually changed.

Maybe it's my fault, but I don't know. She and I got together when she was a virgin. She wanted me to be her first. We talked about using protection, or I would pull my dick out. For some reason, I thought I had that kind of control.

We went to a hotel and lay in bed nervously, both of us. I tried not to let it show. Yvonne wouldn't notice anyway because this was her first time with a man.

Again, my dick acted up, it wouldn't get hard, but my stupid ass came inside of her with a soft dick. I was so naïve that I thought it wasn't enough to get her pregnant, but damn, was I in for some news.

Yvonne kept getting sicker by the week. We both were scared as hell. I didn't know what to do or say, so she finally said she would go to her doctor. There was no way that she could be pregnant because I wasn't even hard.

I was a young fool trying to embrace manhood. Now, circumstances have arrived that will make me a man much quicker. When I found out that Yvonne was pregnant, I was hurt, and I was devastated. How could I be so irresponsible? She was just a virgin, and this was her first time.

## WHAT IT TAKES TO BE THE MAN

We talked about it for hours and finally knew we had to grow up fast. We had a kid on the way. Yvonne immediately started looking for an apartment. I promised to take care of her and the child. I thought I was ready, but life always throws curveballs.

Just in time, I lost my job. Now, how was I going to take care of my new family? I did what I always did: I got back into selling drugs. I only did it briefly, and once again, I found another job.

At that time, Ella and her family came back home. I saw them, and they were one big family. She had two boys and one girl. They said they would stay in Rochester, New York, for about five years and would then be shipped to North Carolina.

I introduced Yvonne to my family at that time. Everyone was happy about Yvonne and me having a baby. It felt good to know that I was going to be a Dad. Then I thought, I don't know the first thing about being a Father. No one taught me to be a Father, and parenting never came with instructions.

Ready or not, my baby was coming, and it would be a boy. I was delighted about that. I talked Yvonne into naming him after me. When the time came, I was in the room with her as she went through her contractions. It didn't take long before she had our son. I know one thing, Yvonne kicked my ass in that delivery room. I got slapped, punched, scratched, and called all kinds of son-of-a-bitches.

## WHAT IT TAKES TO BE THE MAN

It was worth it because I got to be in the room while my son was born. He was a little guy, around six pounds and eight ounces. I was elated and thought I was ready for what was yet to come. I took care of Yvonne and my son for a year while Yvonne was on social services, getting food stamps and government assistance.

After a while, she wanted to get a job, but first, we needed a babysitter. Her Aunt opened up a daycare and said she would take care of Jr. All the years I had been working, I wasn't paid well, but as soon as Yvonne started working, she was paid almost three times more than I was, which became a problem. It was okay for me to take care of her, but she had a problem taking care of me.

Arguments grew between us about money, but on top of that, I kept getting fired from job after job. It seemed as if those white folks had something against me because of my skin color, so what was I to do?

Amid that, Yvonne found herself pregnant again. This time, we found out it would be a girl. I was always against having a daughter. I often prayed that I would never have one, but God had other plans.

The day she had our daughter, something changed in me. I became so in love with that little girl; she was my heart and joy. I no longer wished that I didn't have daughters. How stupid of me to wish and pray such a thing.

## WHAT IT TAKES TO BE THE MAN

I was forced to get two jobs because my money barely scratched the surface, so Yvonne paid most of the bills. She didn't like that very much.

Things changed after my daughter. According to Yvonne, I was a broke son-of-a-bitch, and I couldn't keep a job. I often mentioned how I cared for her and our son when she wasn't working. Those things would have been long forgotten if I had left it up to her.

I soon was fed up with all the arguing. I hated for our two children to hear and to see us argue. I tried to stay with her because I didn't want to leave my children, but I couldn't tolerate the disrespect anymore, and soon it came to a head. I prayed that I would withstand the mental abuse, so I wouldn't leave my children, but how much can a man take?

Yvonne became physical with me one evening. I kept trying to keep her from hurting me. I blocked her punches, her kicks, and her trying to scratch and bite me. That was the last straw. I started packing all of my clothes and taking them to my car. My daughter, Imani, and son, Jr., begged me not to leave, but I felt I had no choice.

They were screaming and crying while Yvonne was cursing me out and, at the same time, trying to make me stay. She said, "These bitches will treat you like shit and throw your broke ass away; anyway, you are going to end up with lots of children with these trifling ass bitches, you will see," I looked at her with disbelief.

## WHAT IT TAKES TO BE THE MAN

Other women weren't even on my mind; I just wanted peace. That evening, I packed my car and left broken-hearted to the core. I always said that no matter what, I would stay in the relationship for my children.

As I pulled away and watched my children cry, I promised myself I would always be in their lives. I didn't know what that would consist of, especially knowing that Yvonne could be a very bitter woman with a vendetta.

Tears ran down my cheeks, and I could see my children crying as I drove off. I didn't have anywhere to go. I was lost and I didn't think this whole thing out. I found myself at Momma's house.

By then, Momma and Dad had split up but were still married. Momma told me that Auntie Ella and her family were leaving town again. I didn't get a chance to see them before they left, but I heard they had a lot of money now.

Momma and I started getting into arguments because she was dating a lazy man, but she and Dad were still married. At this time, Dad had finally found a new girlfriend. It was said that Dad's girl was a crackhead. At the time, I didn't have a clue who she was.

I left Momma's house after we couldn't get along. I felt she showed that lazy nigga more love than she showed me; maybe I had some more growing up to do.

## WHAT IT TAKES TO BE THE MAN

Momma and I didn't talk for a while. I went to stay with Dad and his girlfriend. His girlfriend was nice to me and made me uncomfortable when she always said how handsome I was. I laughed it off, and so did my Dad. I took it as a little disrespectful, but Dad was amused. I kept to myself.

One day, Yvonne called me and said she needed to talk to me about something. I hadn't spoken to her for a while and missed my children. After she put them on the phone and let me talk to them, she dropped a bomb on me.

"I am pregnant with your babies, but I know we aren't together; I think I am getting an abortion," An abortion for what, and what do you mean, babies?" I asked. "I am pregnant with twins," "How do you know? Are you that far along?" "Maybe I am, but I still have enough time to get rid of them," "Hey, don't do that," "Why not? We aren't getting back together," "How do you know that?" "You are over there, or wherever you are at; it doesn't make sense you have all these children by you, and you are not here," "Please, don't get an abortion; there is a chance that we will get back together," I said.

I found out that my pleading didn't even matter. Yvonne had the abortion anyway. I was so damn mad because I didn't have a say so in my own children' lives. Twins, she aborted my twins. Anger filled my heart for a while. I would cry and pray at night, but what was done was done. It took me a long time to get back together with Yvonne.

## WHAT IT TAKES TO BE THE MAN

You can say I started feeling bad for Yvonne because, years later, we found our way back to each other.

Once again, she was pregnant. She said she didn't want to keep the baby, and I begged her not to have another abortion, but she went against my wishes and had another one.

I was devasted, which made things worse for the two of us. Yvonne's old ways came out because of my attitude towards her. I was against abortions, but she eventually killed my unborn children. She started cursing me out and trying to fight me constantly.

I couldn't take it anymore, so I left her and the children again. I never thought Yvonne would find another man by leaving this time, but she did.

At the same time, I also found a girlfriend, Tessa. Tessa was very jealous, especially regarding my children. She didn't want me to spend time with them. I told her, "No matter what you say, I love my children, and you don't tell me when and when I can't spend time with them."

That pissed her off, and it put a wedge and strain on our relationship. We were having good and exciting sex at first, but once she showed her true colors, my dick started acting up again. It wouldn't get hard for her, and she would begin to back away from me. I later found out that she cheated on me with a guy I grew up with. I left her trifling ass alone. I felt relieved because I couldn't stand when she was jealous of my children. What type of woman does that?

One evening, I received a phone call from Yvonne telling me to meet her at the hospital. I was devastated, and I started crying as she told me that my daughter had fallen down the basement stairs and needed stitches.

I nearly killed myself as I found my way to the emergency. My daughter was so happy to see me. She held me so tight. I later found out that Yvonne left my children with her new boyfriend, and my daughter fell into the basement and down all of those stairs. I was pissed as my daughter had twelve stitches on the forehead. That was a scar that would be there for life. How could she let this happen?

After that, things took a turn for the worse. Yvonne and I grew further apart. I was learning lessons, and I had to embrace manhood now. Even through the most traumatic times, I had to stand tall and face everything that was thrown at me —at least, I thought I could, but that remains to be seen.

# Chapter 5

## *Dating A Married Woman*

I walked out of Yvonne's life but tried my best not to walk out of my children's lives. No lie, she made it hard for me at times, but I continued to step up and show my children their Father loved them.

In the midst of that, I was still trying to find myself in a world that made it hard for young black men. I constantly thought of how I could make a change, but something about those streets always seemed to drag me back in.

I kept going through job after job to no avail; I sometimes ended up broke and hungry. There was always that friend who led me back to selling drugs. I didn't want to because I saw what the street did to some of my brothers.

# WHAT IT TAKES TO BE THE MAN

I lost several friends in the drug game. My friends were either murdered or sent to prison. I didn't want to be a statistic, so I kept a low profile when I did what I did.

All that surviving and struggling made me lonely at night. I couldn't believe I let Yvonne go and be with another man. It always played in the back of my mind, so I set out to find myself someone to sleep with at night.

When you're young and dumb, time after time, you will do some stupid shit. I thought it would be good to date a married woman because I wouldn't have to be committed to her, and I could still handle my business, but, damn, was I wrong.

One night, after making some money, I decided to go to the neighborhood bar. It was convenient because I loved to drink, but I hated to drink and drive, so I walked there.

The night was going well, and I danced most of the night. I drank Hennessy and coke, and that shit had me going. I think I was feeling myself. One night, a young lady and her friend approached me and started dancing. I was vibing, and I believed they were feeling my swag.

As the night ended, I got enough heart to ask the thick one her name. Tabitha Miller Quincy was her name. "Why is your name so long? You must be married or something," I said. "I am," "Say what, are you for real?" I said in shock. Man, she was fine and thick with ass and hips. I wanted that ass badly. I couldn't believe she was married so I asked her about five more times. Her friend Tahja J. repeatedly vouched for her, "Yes, that's my girl. She is married and a lawyer," Tahja J. said proudly. "Really?" I asked with a grin. "Girl, stop telling my business; see, I hate when people tell my business, girl, you talk too damn much," Tabitha said jokingly. "Girl, please," Tahja J. said with a smile.

We started walking towards the door because everyone was leaving or, should I say, told to leave by those big-ass bouncers who were undercover police.

"Do you want her number?" Tahja J. said. "She can't give me her number; she's married," I said as I walked close behind them.

"Who said I can't? I am a grown-ass woman," Tabitha said.

"Okay, grown-ass woman, give me your phone, and you better not let your husband find it," I said while Tahja J. chuckled.

"What's so funny?" I asked Tahja J. "I am not in this," She said as she walked ahead of us.

"Are you sure?" I asked when I grabbed her phone.

"Don't you worry about me; worry about your woman or the other women you are sleeping with," Tabitha said with sarcasm.

## WHAT IT TAKES TO BE THE MAN

"I am single, no women here," I said as we exchanged numbers.

"Get that big ole booty; you are going to ride all of that ass, aren't you?" Tahja J. said with a smile.

"Girl shut up and worry about who you're fucking," Tabitha said to Tahja J. "You ladies are a mess," I said as we hugged and went our separate ways.

I admit I thought I was doing something by talking to another man's wife. I didn't realize the magnitude until things got deeper. The very first time I slept with Tabitha, I was nervous that my dick wouldn't get up, but it did. I guess because I was extra excited, I don't know, but I tore that big ass up that night.

I don't know how she escaped her husband that night, but she must have told a good lie. At the time, I found another job and stopped selling drugs. I saved up enough to find an apartment near Tabitha's office, where she was working.

She came to see me every chance that she got. I was in those panties every chance I got until one day, I received a phone call. "Hello, is this DeVon?" I didn't know the voice, so I answered," "Who wants to know?" "Are you fucking my wife?" I got silent. "Nigga, are you fucking my wife?" "No, man, hell no, who is this?" "This is Tabitha's husband, Big Dan; you know who the fuck this is," "I don't know you, and I don't know any, Tabitha," I said, and I quickly slammed the phone. I specifically told that woman not to let her Husband get my number. How did he get my number? I hope she didn't give it to her.

The next time I talked to Tabitha, she told me not to worry about it because her husband was jealous. She said he went through her phone. He suspects something, but he was fishing to see if you took the bait, and you didn't; we have to be more careful,"

I was alarmed at how nonchalant she was, especially when that man called himself Big Dan. That shit scared the hell out of me because I am little DeVon, shit. I thought to myself.

I asked Tabitha repeatedly why she cheats on her husband, and she said that he can't have sex, but other than that, he takes good care of her. "I kind of understand the not having sex part, but if he's a good man and you two said vows, then why not stick with him through whatever problems he's having?" I asked.

"Don't worry about my husband, worry about pleasing me; I need you to fuck me now," She said.

Like a fool, I laid her on the bed and gave her the business. I fucked her until she had three orgasms in a row. As she was leaving my apartment, she said, "You better not sleep with anyone else," I laughed at her, but she was dead serious.

## WHAT IT TAKES TO BE THE MAN

I would ride around the city and see Tabitha and Big Dan driving in their luxurious burgundy Mercedes. They looked happy to me. A couple of times, she saw me, but he didn't. I wonder, how long could I keep this shit up? It wasn't cool anymore, and my consciousness started getting the best of me.

Two weeks later, Big Dan called again threateningly. He cursed me out for interfering in his marriage, and I cursed him out and told him he was talking to the wrong man. Yes, I lied, but he still wasn't buying it.

I talked to Tabitha about him calling me again, and she said he never said anything to her about her cheating or him going through her phone. She turned towards me and said, "Are you sure that's my husband Dan calling you?" I was surprised when she asked me that. It felt as if she was saying that I was fucking someone else wife, and that pissed me off.

"Of course, that's your jealous ass husband; I am not sleeping with anybody else, so I don't know what you are trying to say," Tabitha got quiet, and then she grabbed my zipper to my pants and dropped down to her knees, pulled out my dick and started sucking on it. I gave little resistance, but the shit started feeling good, and just like that, I lost my train of thought.

## WHAT IT TAKES TO BE THE MAN

Tabitha only did this to shut up so I could forget about it. At that moment, my mind was racing, but after she finished, I was not at ease at all. I felt like she was trying to put me in harm's way on purpose.

Big Dan sounded like he would kill anyone if they talked to his wife. I started looking at things differently, like, is this shit worth my life? I didn't want to be one of those guys who gets murdered over someone else's wife.

I slowly backed off Tabitha, and I saw less of her. She complained about it but would show up unannounced when I didn't see her. Some days, I would let her knock loudly, kick my door, and ring the hell out of my doorbell. Some nights, she would be relentless; other times, she would sit by my door crying.

Tabitha was starting to get unstable, and I noticed toxic traits. She began acting as if I were doing her wrong, and I had to keep repeatedly telling her that she was married. My words weren't sinking in her head. I started feeling like I would never get rid of her.

While going through this, the drama started messing with my mental health. All I wanted was a little fun and to get involved with somebody who didn't need a commitment, but this became more of a problem.

For Weeks, Big Dan called my phone. I started to change my number, but I realized that if I gave it to her, he would call that number, too. I thought about blocking him and blocking her, but she was aggressive and unpredictable, and I didn't know what to do. I couldn't call the police because what would I say, "Hey, I am only fucking his wife, man?" I would look stupid as hell. I thought, how do I break this shit off?

Surely enough, the ending was nearing. I started noticing that I was being followed. I kept seeing Big Dan's Mercedes following me from afar. That shit scared the hell out of me, so I started carrying my pipe in my car. I warned my cousins what was going on with me, and they just laughed and told me that's what I get for fucking someone else's wife.

I felt embarrassed, but I had to protect myself. Even when I got off work, I would see that damn Mercedes from afar. I cut off all ties with Tabitha at this point. She was becoming more of a problem than the answer.

I noticed little things started happening, like, little scratch marks on my car and tires going down for no reason, but I couldn't blame her, but shit was suspicious.

While sitting at the red light one evening, Big Dan pulled up next to me. I looked over to my left, and he slowly pulled a pistol from his lap. I hurriedly turned my head, and I ran that damn red light.

## WHAT IT TAKES TO BE THE MAN

That was the last straw. I changed my phone number, and within a few weeks, my lease was up; I moved out and got as far away from Tabitha as possible.

I feared for my life, and this wasn't a game anymore, and once again, I had to quit my job because that Mercedes kept showing up. Yvonne started yelling and cursing me out because I couldn't pay the child support.

I had to resort to street survival to ensure my children had food and clothing. I did what I had to do, and I did what any real man would do: I got money in any way that I could.

After leaving that job and changing my phone number, I stopped seeing Tabitha and didn't see that Mercedes. I stayed out of their way. I knew soon she would find another man and put his life in danger because she didn't care about my safety.

From that day forth, messing around with a married woman was not in my playbook. I could've gotten myself killed over another man's wife. I thought I had to stop doing this because I would not want another man sleeping with my future wife.

Sometimes, karma comes, and that's one of the things that made me open my eyes. It wasn't a good thing to do. After months, I realized I had made the right choice because Big Dan ended up on the news. Tabitha put another man's life in jeopardy, and Big Dan shot that man and was now facing ten to twenty-five years in jail. That was a close call because, at any time, that could've been me. Now, Tabitha will go on with her life and sleep with someone else while another man rots in jail and the other man rots in hell or his grave.

Being a man comes with challenges, and I have had many. Through this journey, I realized that my life was meaningful to myself and my children.

I knew I needed to make the best decisions in the future, so my mission was just that. No one ever said it was easy being a man, so I had to evolve as my experiences molded me to try to be a better man and mold me into a better version of myself.

# Chapter

# 6

## *Going backwards*

After all that chaotic shit went down, I did what any normal man would do, and that was to converse with my Momma. For some reason, she helped me look at things differently and for the better,

Momma gave me some startling news while we were conversing. "Your Aunt Ella and her husband Carlton are hooked on drugs," "Say what, do you mean smoking too much weed?" "Worse, I heard they were smoking crack cocaine," That news shocked me because, from my hindsight, they were living the good life. "What about her children?" I asked with curiosity. "So far, as I know, they are okay, but he has been kicked out of the service," Momma said. I couldn't believe what I was hearing. All I could think of at this point was, wow, God is

## WHAT IT TAKES TO BE THE MAN

going to put a whipping on her because of what she did to me as a child.

"What are you thinking about?" Momma asked.

"Oh, nothing," I said as I kept it to myself.

We changed subjects even though I found Auntie Ella's path quite interesting. I told Momma about the married woman, and she was distraught. I promised her that I wouldn't engage in anything like that anymore.

When she found out that Big Dan was the man who shot a man over his wife, she nearly slapped me out of me silly. I had to make that promise because that little slap across my head hurt.

I left Momma's house as soon as her boyfriend came home. For some reason, I didn't like that man. He wasn't working, and he loved to smoke lots of marijuana. He spoke as I walked out of the house, but I just looked his sorry ass up and down. Now, why would Momma be with a man who can't work? I guess he was getting a disability check; that was his situation; hell, he looked healthy to me.

I finally found a new, good-paying job with benefits, so I was ready to take on the world now. I knew Yvonne would love that I would be able to give her more money for the children.

Weeks later, after living in hotels, I found another apartment. This time, it was far away from the neighborhood where I sold drugs. I didn't want to do the street shit anymore; I wanted to be a man and handle my business the legal way.

After being single for months, somehow, Yvonne and I started calling and texting each other on the phone. It started with talking about our children and then us trying to hook up.

You see, Yvonne still had a new boyfriend, and he was younger than her. I remember asking her what happened to the guy she was with who let my daughter fall down the basement stairs, and she told me about the clown.

She was so open to me that it nearly broke my heart; it made me wonder why, in the hell, I would let my virgin children's Mother go. I don't think she realized that while she was opening up to me, it was something that made me keep my feelings for her to a minimum.

"His name was Dwayne, and he was a lot different than you were with me in bed; his thing was kind of small, so all he wanted to do was go down on me and lick my cooty cat," Yvonne said.

"Oh, that's it, huh?" I said with anguish.

"Yeah, it wasn't much, but I did love it when he did that; it felt real good, but that's about it. I mean, you are excellent in bed, don't get me wrong, but you and I didn't go down on each other, maybe because we were young," Yvonne said.

"Yes, we both were young, but I don't have any problem with that now," I said.

"No, I wouldn't want you to do that to me; we're good just having normal sex. I think he only did that because he knew his thing was little; I mean, our son's little dick was just as big as his," She giggled.

I tried to laugh because it was funny, but damn, he strung her ass out with his tongue. I knew at that moment that I needed to boost up my sex game. I couldn't let that bit of information slide. I didn't want to give another man the edge on me in my sex game.

"So, what's up with this new boyfriend of yours?" I asked as if I wanted to know.

"His name is Saban, he's young, he's okay, but he's not you,"

"Well, that's a good thing, so when will I see you again?"

"You mean to have sex?" She chuckled.

I laughed and said, "I am just asking because I sometimes miss you." "I miss you too; let me see when I can sneak away," She said.

Finally, weeks later, we managed to get together, and we made passionate love. I wanted to go down on her, but the way she described how Dwayne licked her up and down, I was afraid that I wouldn't be able to compete. I knew that was something I was going to need to practice. I could tell she didn't want us to do that to each other, but I didn't understand.

She snuck away on occasions after that. Then, one day, we stopped calling each other. Months later, I found out that Yvonne was pregnant. I am not going to lie; that shit hurt me like hell.

A part of me wanted to hate her and be a bitter man, but she had my two children, and as a man, I couldn't be that way, not alone let my children see that side of me, so I stayed cordial.

While Yvonne was pregnant, I would go and get my children and sometimes keep them with me. One evening after I dropped them off, I pulled to the corner of the street, and I heard several loud noises and flashing lights coming in my direction, so I immediately ducked down in my seat.

I looked up, and a car pulled off quickly. Shots rang out from a gun. I was scared as hell. I wasn't sure if those bullets were for me, but I got the hell out of that area.

I had no enemies except Big Dan, who threatened me on my phone. And, as far as I knew, he was in jail. I was paranoid or something. I was the only car on that corner, and that car took off fast.

I was shaking, and I was scared. I believe that taught me not to ever talk to another married woman.

## WHAT IT TAKES TO BE THE MAN

One day after that, I ran into Tabitha, and she confirmed what I already knew. She said Big Dan's brother admitted to shooting at me.

I knew it, but that confirmation was all I needed. I could've turned his brother into the police, but where I am from, we don't snitch to the police. Tabitha wouldn't be a witness for me anyway.

She had the nerve to try to hook up with me, and I turned her down. I just left it at that and went on about my business. I was paranoid everywhere I went until I ran into Tabitha's friend, Tahja J.

"You know Tabitha is divorcing Big Dan?" She said as we talked in front of the convenience store.

"Well, he is locked up in jail," I said.

"He's going through some health issues; I think he has cancer and some heart problems; while he's locked up, you better go get your girl back,"

"She's not my girl. I am sorry for them, but I am not putting myself back into that with your girl,"

"I understand, believe me, I understand, but that's my girl. I will tell her. I saw you. Take it easy," She said as she jumped into her car and pulled off.

## WHAT IT TAKES TO BE THE MAN

I didn't know what to think about the information she gave me, but I knew one thing, I wasn't getting back into that crazy shit, hell, that man could've killed me, but it's a good thing he's locked up.

I sat quietly in my apartment, thinking about the next move in my life. What was next? As of now, I have kept my new job, but I am lonely. The only times I felt complete were whenever I got the chance to see my children.

I wanted them to be proud of me even though they were young. I wanted to be the best Father I could be, even if it meant their Mother and I wouldn't reunite.

After a while, loneliness took over, so I started meeting new friends, which meant new women. I decided to entertain myself with a Latina woman named Maritza.

Maritza was very friendly, and she loved to cook. We got along incredibly. She was a kind, free-spirited woman, and I loved that about her. She was always busy, so we didn't see each other much, but we made the best of it when we did.

I admired how hardworking she was. She had her home, but two of her children lived with her. They were nice to me, and I liked them. The time we spent together was incredible. Maritza helped me see things in another way.

## WHAT IT TAKES TO BE THE MAN

I always sought advice from her, especially regarding my children. Over time, we became good friends. Her schedule as a nurse didn't allow anything else.

Slowly, we grew apart. Even the intimacy had slipped away. It was one of those things where we respected each other too much to take a chance and ruin such a great friendship.

I never had any bad feelings; we just enjoyed the little time that life gave us. She disappeared from my life after a while, and our lives went in two different directions.

I heard she had gotten married. That was odd because she was always a busy woman. It wasn't meant to be. It's funny how things change in the blink of an eye.

At this point, it felt like I couldn't keep a relationship, so I had to reflect on my life's choices. I wasn't sure of myself anymore. I didn't have the answers, so I needed to talk to someone that did.

"Momma, I need to talk to you,"

"That's the only time that you call me,"

"No, stop that, Momma, you know I love you,"

"I love you too, but do you call your Dad?"

## WHAT IT TAKES TO BE THE MAN

"No, not really; Dad doesn't like to talk about women and sex; he acts like he's scared or something," "That man isn't scared of anything, the way he cheated on me," She said.

I couldn't help but reflect on the time I saw her cheating on Dad when I was little. I just kept my remarks to myself. I told her about my love life, and I told her about Yvonne being pregnant.

Momma didn't care much for Yvonne then, so she gave me great advice. "Move on with your life, and I believe that damn girl is crazy anyway,"

I must admit she is a bit crazy, but she is the Mother of my children,"

"Yes, that's true, but any woman you choose can be the Mother of your children; it's all about who you choose, and somehow, you chose that crazy ass girl,"

"Momma, what's done is done, now about my love life,"

"You are a grown man, you have to figure that shit out for yourself, but I will tell you this, make sure you stay in your children's life; they must see that they have a Dad who cares,"

"I am doing exactly that, but now that Yvonne is having a child with another guy, there might be some drastic changes,"

# WHAT IT TAKES TO BE THE MAN

"I don't care about how drastic the changes are; you just be there and don't let another man watch my grandchildren; if you ever need me, just call me, and I will watch them," Momma said.

We conversed for hours. I finally got what I came for: to talk to someone. Momma helped me look at things in a different light. Most of the things I already knew, but it was good to get confirmation.

# Chapter 7

## *Dealing With A Nightmare*

Months later, Yvonne had a baby girl. I was happy for her but also hurt and a bit jealous. I thought I would be the only man she would have children with, but life always throws us a curve ball.

In the midst of that, Momma called me one night, crying very wildly and loudly. "Momma, what's going on?" I yelled.

"This son-of-a-bitch and I got into a fight, and now I am in the hospital," "What do you mean that you're in the hospital, Momma? What happened?" I asked anxiously.

"He's a jealous asshole, he got upset because a man I knew way back from school spoke to me, and he smiled,"

"What happened then? What hospital are you at?"

## WHAT IT TAKES TO BE THE MAN

"I am at General Hospital. We got into a fight, and he punched me in my mouth, and he knocked my three front teeth out of my mouth,"

"What? He is going to die, "I yelled out.

"DeVon, calm down, he is going to pay, believe me, I can't believe what he did to me," She screamed as she cried.

"Momma, Momma, where is that coward? I am going to fuck his ass up. Does Dad know?"

"No, he doesn't, and don't tell him either,"

"What, I have to tell Dad, and I am calling my cousins and my friends; we are going to kick his ass for this," I yelled.

"Come to the hospital now, and I don't want you to get into any trouble,"

"Momma, it's too late for that, and you said he knocked out your front teeth; oh hell no, his ass is done when I see him,"

"DeVon, DeVon, wait until I get out," She cried.

"No, I can't wait; you said your teeth are out too," I yelled.

"I have insurance. The doctor will give me three false teeth,"

"Hell, no, talk to you later, Momma,"

"DeVon, DeVon, DeVon, no," She screamed, but I hung up. I immediately called Dad first and told him what had happened. "Say what, he did what, oh shit, I knew this would happen, see I would never lay a hand on your Momma; I knew these crazy men wouldn't take what I took from her in our marriage," He said.

"I am not getting in your and Momma's business, but when I catch that man, he's going to get it,"

"DeVon, calm down; I don't want you to kill him or go to jail,"

"Dad, there isn't any calming down. He hit my Momma, and he knocked out three of her front teeth,"

"What?" Dad said inquisitively. "Yes, Dad, now I am going to knock him out,"

"Oh my God," "I am not playing Dad," "I understand, son, if that were my Momma, I would feel the same way, just don't get yourself in jail, please stay out of harm's way,"

"Right now, I can't care about me; that's my Momma,"

"You are right, you only get one,"

"I am calling up my friends and a few cousins, but first, I am headed to the hospital. Are you coming?"

"No, you keep me in touch; this is a shame. I warned your Momma long ago; do you know what their fight was about?"

## WHAT IT TAKES TO BE THE MAN

"I have to go, Dad; I will fill you in later." "Okay, please be careful; I love you, son," He said as we hung up the phone.

I called everyone, and they all met me at the hospital. I cried when I saw my Momma without all her teeth. I held her tightly. After we left Momma's room, we plotted how we would get that son-of-a-bitch back.

I was so irate and didn't care how I got him back. I was on a mission, and my life didn't come first; my Momma did. We were about to leave the hospital, but I heard Momma call out to me, so I ran back into her room while everyone discussed shit outside of her hospital room.

"Look, son, I love you, and I know what you plan on doing, but please don't kill him; I don't want to see you in jail,"

"But Momma," "Promise me, you won't kill him, promise me," She said aggressively. I didn't say a word, but the doctor interrupted us. They were talking Momma out to fix her teeth.

I walked out of the hospital to look for the coward. Let's just say when we caught him, he got the beating of his damn life. I almost killed that damn man; well, I could, but I remembered what Momma and Dad said. I believe I just gave his ass a wake-up call.

I worried about him and his family retaliating against me, but that never happened. I believe I put the fear of God in him. After a few

## WHAT IT TAKES TO BE THE MAN

months, Momma was back to herself, and things were back to normal. Her false teeth looked just like the ones she had before.

I watched over her for a while to make sure she was safe, and she was. We never heard from that asshole again, and that was a good thing.

Often, I sat at home and had these nightmares. I could see myself getting shot or killed. Those nightmares bother me deeply. I don't know what God or those nightmares were telling me, but I felt it wasn't anything good.

As soon as life was calm again, I got the shock of my life, and it wasn't what a Father ever wants to hear.

"DeVon, please come to the hospital," Yvonne screamed. I could tell she was crying. "What's wrong with you, woman? What happened?"

"It's your daughter, Imani; a pitbull attacked her, and she might die," "What, what, pitbull, she might die?" I screamed as tears started flowing out of the wells of my eyes,

"Yes, she was mauled by one of the neighbor's dogs,"

"What, no, no, how? Who was she with, and where is that dog?"

"She was walking to the supermarket with my boyfriend when the dog came out and attacked them,"

# WHAT IT TAKES TO BE THE MAN

Where was he?" I heard that he ran and left her," "What the fuck did you say, that muthafucka left my daughter to be mauled?"

"Yes, that's what I heard. Come to Genesee Hospital; your daughter needs you now," She said while crying.

I jumped off my bed, put on my clothes, and went to the hospital. I couldn't keep my composure when I walked into Imani's room.

Imani lay in the bed with tubes down her throat and needles in her arm while her body was stitched up from head to toe. It felt as if those nightmares had come to life.

I pondered on the fact that my nightmares were telling me something, but I couldn't understand them. I felt helpless as Imani lay in the bed unconsciously. My son, Jr. walked in with his Auntie, and I hugged him. We both cried.

That experience alone changed me. I felt helpless, and my daughter's life hung in the balance. It was good that God answered my prayers because Imani woke up days later and started showing improvement.

It is so wild how things can change so quickly and unexpectedly. The doctor said Imani will heal, but some of those scars will be on her body for life. I prayed to God and wished to take Imani's place, but it wasn't meant for me. My daughter was strong, and she fought with the help of therapy. I was so happy that she lived through such a torturous ordeal. I promised her and God that I would watch over her better.

I wanted to be a better version of a Father to both of my children. I knew that came with changes in my life. Even though I tried to kill Yvonne's boyfriend for running off and leaving Imani like that, I believe God didn't put it in my heart to get revenge.

I am not saying I didn't try to catch him and kick his ass, and it's just I couldn't find him and catch him alone. His cowardly ass must have left the state because he wasn't anywhere to be found. That was a good thing.

The negative thoughts left my mind because I knew my daughter needed me during her healing. I guess during this period, I was left open to vulnerability.

I met a sweet woman named Sheronda McMillan at my job. She was new, so I showed her around. Once I told her about my daughter's condition, we immediately became close. Sheronda was a shoulder to lean on; she helped me get through so many rough patches in my life.

The way she looked at me and talked to me told a story. I could see she was authentic and very sincere. As the days went by, we grew closer.

We finally admitted to each other that we found one another attractive. It was unbelievable because Sheronda finished my sentences, could sense when I was upset or something was bothering me, and loved to make me smile.

I needed all those things in a woman and my life. Sheronda was a rare breed. Even though I didn't want to admit it to myself or her, I fell in love with her from the start.

They say loneliness and vulnerability can do that to a person, especially to someone who went through something traumatic, such as what happened to Imani. Whatever it was, I felt like I was in a good place.

We started dating, and she loved my children. I felt sorry for her because a doctor told her that she couldn't have any babies, and that's why she was so close to mine.

We often had intense conversations about why she couldn't conceive. "I always wanted children, but that was taken from me," She said faintly. "What do you mean, what happened?" "I am not sure, and the doctor said the problems could've stemmed from being oversexed,

"What does that mean?" "It means, at a young age, I was having sex with older men, and maybe one of them gave me an STD that made me sterile or I can't conceive." "Did he really tell you that?" "Yes, is so many words," "Did you have a second opinion?" "I have had several; I just gave up; it's okay because now I have your children," She said with a smile.

## WHAT IT TAKES TO BE THE MAN

The way Sheronda looked at life made my heart smile. Everything was for a reason and in a positive light. I was pleased that God brought her into my life.

I was getting so comfortable with having Sheronda in my life, but like always, life shows you that you're not in control.

I received a call one evening, and it broke my heart. Sheronda died of a heart attack while in her bathroom, getting ready for work. I left work in a hurry. I nearly had one just thinking about her.

She had so much more life to live, and she brought me out of my dark space in just a short time. I wish I had one last time to tell her I appreciated and loved her.

Sheronda was taken away from me in just a blink of an eye. My heart sank low. I was a stranger to her family at her funeral, but a couple of them knew what she meant to me because she told them, and they told me.

At that time, I felt my life would never be the same, and I felt cheated. Why did this happen to such a beautiful person? Bad things always happen to good people.

How can I bounce back after this loss? Life is full of pain, but I guess this was just another test of my manhood. The tears flowing out of my eyes left a stain on my heart, which bothered my mind.

# WHAT IT TAKES TO BE THE MAN

The loss of Sheronda made me want to achieve more, and be a shoulder and a crutch to others in need.

Sheronda was an extraordinary woman, and she will never be forgotten. You can say she is my angel up in heaven. Thank you, baby, I always say as I pray. This life isn't easy!

# Chapter 8

## *The Beginning Of Change*

At a time when I felt like I had no one, my parents were there for me. Momma and Dad always asked about one another, which I found interesting.

I told them to leave me out of it, pick up the phone, and talk to each other. Since they were both there for me, they eventually started seeing each other again.

The time apart from each other was a significant factor. My Momma had changed, and so did Dad. They both outgrew each other, and it showed.

## WHAT IT TAKES TO BE THE MAN

They would have little arguments, leading to Dad leaving the house and not returning. Sometimes, you can't fix what's broken. After a while, they just became friends again.

Truthfully, I never understood their relationship. They were married but lived as singles. I prayed that wouldn't happen to me, but life has its paths sometimes.

It's funny how life leaves you in limbo, and you feel trapped in your circumstances. I could feel my mind maturing and changing. Thoughts of being something other than a man who works for different people made me think I should be in charge of my destiny, but how? Who am I to this vast world?

I was at a point where I didn't know who I was. I sat in my apartment every evening and began writing down a plan. I started watching TV and movies more.

It was unbelievable how I knew what the plot would be in the movies that I watched. I wanted to write a movie. I was messing around, but I tried daily.

Finally, I decided to join a college that could teach me how to write. After I learned all the information, I was told I would have to hold out until the following semester, which was the following year.

## WHAT IT TAKES TO BE THE MAN

I was excited about that. While I waited until the upcoming Fall, I practiced and watched tutorial after tutorial, and I never told a soul—not even my children knew.

It was all work and no play for a while, and once again, I found myself lonely and wanting a woman to share my life with. I will try one more time to find the love of my life.

Losing Sheronda to a heart attack was hard, but I was human, and my body ached for another female soul to connect with. While I was sorrowful, a woman named Drea Watson entered my life.

Drea was half Jamaican and American but lived through her Jamaican heritage. She had a powerful spirit, strong and independent. I was constantly reminded that she didn't need a man but wanted one.

I couldn't change some of the ways that she looked at life. Deep down, I thought she was a good woman. Our relationship grew, so I stayed at her house most of the time.

When we made love, it was magic. The things we did in the bedroom were unmatched. No one ever made me feel that way as a man. How she made my flesh feel helped me be blind to all the red flags.

When I needed to talk and vent, she would criticize me and put me down instead of listening to me. That was a big turn-off, so we stopped communicating like we once did.

## WHAT IT TAKES TO BE THE MAN

A relationship can't last without communication. Eventually, we started to stray away from one another. Things got worse once I caught her talking to another man.

I pulled them up at the market, and when I got close, I saw them exchange phone numbers. I backed up slowly, and I drove away before she saw me.

I wanted to bring it to her attention, but that little voice inside my head said to let it be. I had been through too much, so I buried my head in my writing.

I got myself a new desktop computer, looked up all the scriptwriting uploads, uploaded the free ones, and taught myself how to write movie scripts.

For many nights, I didn't sleep. Drea would call me, but I stopped all contact, and after a while; I changed my phone number. I thought that would end things between us, but I realized that some women need closure, or they will go crazy on your ass, and that's what happened.

One evening, while getting home from work, I was caught off guard when Drea showed up in a tan trench coat with one arm behind her back.

"Can you just leave me like that rude boy?" She yelled in a heavy Jamaican accent,

## WHAT IT TAKES TO BE THE MAN

"What are you doing here? I want you to leave me alone," I yelled.

"Fuck that, man; no one tells Drea what to do, man; you didn't have the decency to tell me like a man should do?"

"Look, we aren't compatible. I am tired, and I don't think it's in our best interest to stop talking; we can be friends," I said as I headed closer to the front door of my apartment.

"Fuck that shit, rude boy," She said as she pulled out a machete and took a swing at me. I was so agile that I jumped out of the way.

"Bitch are you crazy," I yelled as I ran a little way down the street. "You are about to find out right now, and you got the right woman to play with now; I am not playing with your ass, man, no closure. Is that what you give me?" She said as she swung at me again and again.

All I could think about was my children and how much they needed me. This irrational woman was trying to take my life. I did what every real man would do; I ran. I didn't want to die, and neither did I want to put a hand on a woman.

I could see people riding by, some laughing and some on their cell phones. I couldn't tell if they were calling the police or not, so I yelled, "Call the damn police; this woman is crazy,"

## WHAT IT TAKES TO BE THE MAN

That must have startled Drea because she dropped that machete to her side, ran back the opposite way, and jumped into her car while screaming and yelling, "I will teach your ass for playing with me; this is what you get. Man, I don't play,"

Shortly after she pulled off, the police showed up; I had no words then. I knew that I had to move out of my apartment immediately before that crazy lady came back.

I called my Momma, and I told her what happened, and she was pissed off at me. "You better leave those crazy ass whores alone,"

"I wasn't messing with her, and she just turned crazy on me,"

"Just get your things and get out of there; you can come and stay here for a while, at least until you find another apartment; these women are crazy these days; you can't play with their feelings,"

"Momma, I swear, I wasn't, but I will get my things, and the rest of it I will put into storage," I said as we hung up the phone.

As I was driving, I started getting paranoid because it seemed as if someone was following me. I constantly looked out of my rearview mirror to make sure it wasn't Drea with that damn machete.

When I made it to my Momma's house, I looked both ways as I got out of my car and dodged into her house. "Boy, are you all right?"

"I am now; that damn lady wanted to kill me."

## WHAT IT TAKES TO BE THE MAN

"I've told you a million times, and you can't play with these women's feelings; they will gut you and stab you up; now, suppose she did cut you with that machete; what is your family supposed to do?" "I know, but I wasn't playing with her feelings; I wasn't feeling her anymore; you know how some people give you those vibes like, nope, this isn't the right person? Well, that's how I felt, so I stopped talking to her,"

"That's why she got all crazy; you can't sleep with women and give them good sex in bed and think you can just walk away like that; some women want closure,"

"That's what she said, something about closure, but isn't closure when you back off and stop talking to them? Shouldn't they get the picture?"

"Some will, and some get so attached that they are like, how dare you leave me? You are my possession,"

"Then they have a problem, not me." "Boy, just bring the rest of your things to this house, and let's finish talking," Momma said with a smirk.

I slowly walked outside to get my things and looked both ways. I had to stop laughing because that seemed like something out of a movie. At that very second, it made me think about putting that scene with Drea in a movie script; I thought that would grab some attention.

## WHAT IT TAKES TO BE THE MAN

I opened the car door and saw a car drive by fast, so I hurried, grabbed some of my things, and ran to the house. Momma stood at the door laughing at me. I felt so embarrassed, but hell. Drea was swinging that damn machete at my damn head. I was overly cautious now. "Boy, that woman got your ass scared," Momma said with laughter. "I want to live, Momma, I want to live," I giggled.

Momma and I sat down, and she told me more about Aunt Ella. Aunt Ella and Carlton had gotten into those drugs so severely that they were living out in the streets while their children were staying home alone.

"Where are they now?" I asked. "Carlton is out there doing who knows what, but I think Ella is going crazy; she's out there selling her body, and she knows that she's married,"

"That's insane," "It is, and if she keeps it up, she's going to end up losing her children or, even worse, mess around and get some bad drugs that might mess her brains up,"

"You are right about that," "Enough about your crazy ass family members; I know you are tired; I am going to get you a towel and a washcloth so you can shower,"

"Okay, Momma, I am exhausted." While she went to get my towels, I sat and thought about my Aunt Ella's life; what a turnaround; your life can change instantly.

## WHAT IT TAKES TO BE THE MAN

I couldn't understand why they started doing drugs in the first place. That's not the answer when things are going wrong in your life. I knew that I was too strong to fall into drugs, but I guess for some people, that's the only answer. Momma finally brought my towels, and she said good night and headed to her bedroom.

I sat, and I thought about my life before I went and showered. I could see myself getting tired of relationships and job after job. I needed a change, and I needed one badly.

Creating movie scripts of all the toxic relationships and jobs I've been on would make a great story one day. It was far-fetched, but I made it up in my mind that I would research and learn as much as I could.

After all the thoughts and questions, I went and took my shower. I planned to make a change from that night forward, but that's only if I could stay away from negative people and distractions.

The following day, I went and spent time with my children. Yvonne didn't come out of the house, but I did get a glimpse of Yvonne's baby girl she had. Imani was talking up a storm. I was so happy for her, and her wounds healed very well. You could see some of her scars, but I was so pleased that she was still alive.

My son sat in the front seat smiling. He was happy to be around his Father, and I felt the same way. My children brought me calmness

# WHAT IT TAKES TO BE THE MAN

and made me want to be the best version of myself. I genuinely love my children.

I took them out to eat, and we enjoyed ourselves. My children kept me laughing and smiling. They were my joy, even in the midst of so many storms. As a man and Dad, I wanted to make them both proud.

They were the reason a change had to happen in my life. I owed everything to them.

WHAT IT TAKES TO BE THE MAN

# Chapter

# 9

## *A Heavy Load to Bear*

My job started taking me through hell. Someone was always trying to write me up. I was doing my best, but it wasn't good enough for those people.

It pissed me off how so many people weren't good workers, but because of my color or race, I had to work extra harder. On top of that, with all the troubles that black men have outside of the job, the load begins to get too heavy.

I constantly tried to overlook all the obstacles, but sometimes, enough was enough. During my downtime, I practiced writing movie manuscripts and signed up to attend Movie Script festivals and venues.

## WHAT IT TAKES TO BE THE MAN

Whenever I got the chance, I visited those venues and met some incredible people. I wanted to be fed all the knowledge that I could be fed.

Gracy M. Edwards, the producer of the Movie Why Not Tonight, gave me her card and asked me to send her my manuscript. I was so happy. A few agents also gave me their cards.

Then, when I got back into town, the same headaches hit me as I tried to keep to myself at my job. There was always this bully on the job. It's wild how these bullies never get into trouble.

The more I stayed to myself, the more she tried to push my buttons. I ignored her, but deep down, I was cursing her the hell out. After all the stress at work, some more obstacles came my way.

Yvonne started working, and she would leave my children alone. I had conversations with her about it, and she just talked shit to me about it. I couldn't convince her that leaving them there alone was dangerous. If the wrong people found out, our children could get taken, and that's what I said to her every time.

Yvonne's head was too damn hard, and o couldn't get through to her. Again, all this stress was heavy on my mind. I was ready to explode some days, but my dreams kept me strong and hopeful.

One day, I received a phone call from Momma, and she said Auntie Ella was locked up in a crazy house. I was shocked when I asked, "What is she doing in a crazy house?" "Somebody must have given her some bad drugs because they found her talking to herself, and they locked her ass up," I did know what to think, but sure enough, they locked up and put her on medicines. My cousins and Auntie Ellas' children went to stay with my Grandmother. It was a sad situation. Ella's husband, Carlton, was seen smoking dope in the streets.

I heard he smoked cocaine so much that his bottom lip turned pink. He tried several times to take his children from my Grandmother's house, but she didn't have it.

My Grandmother cursed his ass out and made him leave, and told him, "You need to get your addict ass in rehab when you do that, then you can get these children; you and Ella need to get your shit together,"

Momma told me all about it. Life is hard, and it will make or break you. With everything going on, I tried to keep my stress levels down. After a few months, Momma, Grandmother, and my Uncle Levi went to see Auntie Ella in that mental hospital.

Ella looked like she had lost her mind. Her hair was wild-looking, and she looked like a homeless person. The odor on her body was sickening to my stomach.

## WHAT IT TAKES TO BE THE MAN

I looked at her in disbelief. Flashbacks of her came to me as Momma tried to tell her to get herself together so she could take care of her children. It seemed as if she jumped in and out of the same crazy mental state. It was scary to see her like this.

After we left the hospital, we all concluded that somebody must have poisoned her or given her some harmful drugs. Grandmother prayed for her, and we hoped for the best.

That night, I thought to myself, with all that was happening, that maybe I should write a movie script about Ella's downfall. I will name it, Downfall Disbelief.

The way her life turned out, it had to be a movie. I loaded a program that helped you format movie scripts and began writing her story. I stopped a few hours into the script because it was time to get into bed and get ready for work the following day.

As I woke up that morning, I prayed on the side of my bed. I looked to God to lead me and give me strength from these people at my job. After my shower, I got dressed and headed to work.

That crazy bully named Thelma Cross started cursing at everyone, and she gave me nasty looks. I didn't know her problem, but she didn't like me for any reason. I tried repeatedly to be cordial with her. Some days she would be nice to me, and other days, she would be an asshole. On this day, she was an asshole and a bully. Thelma slammed some long hoses on my tray while I was working. I looked at her and sighed as I talked to God in my head.

These people have a way of making a black man angry and then playing victim, so I had to be mindful of that. I walked away and went to the bathroom to take a breather.

I prayed again, came out, and went back to work. I had my back turned, and suddenly, Thelma appeared. Thelma went into the drawer of my desk and started shooting tools around. I just stared at her, and I shook my head. As she was walking away, I heard her say, "Muthafucker, needs to put my tools back,"

I was so angry that tears came out of my eyes. Once again, I walked away and breathed out to control myself. I prayed to God, and I had hoped that she didn't approach me anymore that day.

Luckily, God must have answered my prayers because she didn't come my way the rest of the day. I was happy because it was a Friday, and by now, I had enough of her shit.

Why do black men have to deal with this kind of shit? I only wanted to come to work to get a paycheck, but somehow, these people find a way to make you into just another nigga.

Just as I thought my weekend would get better, things changed in the blink of an eye. I got off work, showered, and went to get my children so we could spend time with them, but Yvonne said they couldn't come because she didn't have a babysitter.

We argued for a while. "Look, I want to spend time with my children; why can't they come with me?" "I don't have a babysitter, so they can't go anywhere." "Why don't you get someone in your family to watch them?" "You don't think I asked anyone, and they are all too busy,"

"That's not my fault. These are my children, and I want to spend time with them." "Well, you can't." "You know this isn't right." "I don't care; they can't go with you," She yelled.

My son walked down the stairs with his baby sister in his hands. He smiled and handed his sister to Yvonne. He was so happy because he thought he was going with me.

"I don't know why you are smiling, for you can't go with your Dad," Yvonne said. My son immediately started crying.

"See what you have done," I said with crossed arms.

"He better stop crying like a little girl; he isn't grown. I tell him what to do," What she said irked the hell out of me.

"You see, he wants to go," I said.

My son has started screaming. "I want to go with my Dad,"

## WHAT IT TAKES TO BE THE MAN

"Boy, if you don't shut up," Yvonne yelled, and my son ran into the house screaming and crying.

"Shut the hell up, you sound like a little girl," Yvonne yelled. "Listen, stop talking to my son that way, it's okay for him to cry, he is human,"

"He is a boy. And one day he is going to be a man; he can't cry, that is for little girls,"

"Who told you that shit?" I asked.

"Don't curse at me; if you keep talking to me, you won't see either one of your children,"

I paused because a part of me wanted to slap the shit out of her, but I am too much of a man to stoop that low. It's a shame when a woman uses her children as a weapon against you.

I started to walk off her porch, and her baby said, "Bye, Daddy," I was shocked.

"Girl, that isn't your Daddy," Yvonne said in a low voice,

"See what you are starting," I said.

"She's confused because you came to get your son and your daughter; here, do you want to take her too, and that way, you can take your children too?"

## WHAT IT TAKES TO BE THE MAN

"Are you crazy? No, this isn't right," I said as I walked to my car.

"Maybe next time, you can take them; I have to get a babysitter," She said as I pulled off in my car.

The nerve of her asking me to take another man's baby with me and my children. How was that even an option? Some women are crazy about using their children that way.

This was my life. I prayed for changes. Another man would've cursed her out or maybe even taken the children from her in court. My children loved their Mother, so I thought twice before taking that action.

Everywhere I turned, there was a heavy load to bear. People say weathering a storm and a crisis strengthens a man, but I wasn't feeling that strong.

The following weekend I went to get my children; it was the same shit with Yvonne. Again, she asked me to take her baby, which is another man's child. I refused, and I threatened to take her to court. I guess you can say that pissed her off because she threatened to shoot me. I hauled ass in my car.

Later, she called me and apologized. I acted like I accepted her apology, but deep down, that shit pissed me off. I am only trying to get my children to spend time with them. There are so many black men out there who don't give their children the time of day, but I am being punished for wanting to spend time with mine.

The following week, I tried to see my children again, but I found out by Yvonne's family member that she was in the hospital. The new boyfriend dragged her down the street in her car and ran over her right arm.

I searched all over the place for my children, and luckily, they were at her Aunt Catherine's house. I went, and I got my children. While Yvonne was in the hospital, my children stayed with me. My Momma watched them while I was at work,

That time only lasted a few weeks before Yvonne came to get them one day. She had her arm in a sling. I felt terrible for her. Yvonne told me and my Momma the story of that crazy boyfriend of hers getting jealous and nearly killing her in her car.

She was banged up pretty badly. I kissed my children, and they got into her car. The front end of her car was smashed in. I was surprised she was still driving it. "I yelled out, "You better fix that car," "I will, I am," She said. I stood there watching my children look sad as she pulled off. I wished they could live with me forever. Maybe if I became wealthy from selling my movie scripts, I could take my children away from her.

"What are you thinking? Momma asked.

## WHAT IT TAKES TO BE THE MAN

"Oh, nothing, but you see how karma is getting her?"

"Yes, I see, that crazy ass boyfriend of hers almost killed her,"

"Momma, I told her other men aren't as nice as me, and they will hurt her for treating them a certain way,"

"You did, and what did she say?" "She didn't take me seriously; now look, her car is smashed up, and he could've killed her,"

"Well, if he does, that's her life," Momma said. "I know, but that is the Mother of my children," "True, but she doesn't respect you, DeVon," Momma said as she headed back into the house. Momma's words always affected me in the worst way, especially when she was telling me the truth. I didn't want to hear that, but that's life.

Amid all these distractions, I had to try to maintain my sanity. I went to work with the world on my shoulders, yet I had to conduct myself as a strong man without feelings. I tried my best, but one day, my manager pulled out an evil spirit in me.

We were at the end of the work shift, and I had only three minutes to go home, so I stood near my desk with my arms crossed. Out of nowhere, My manager showed up with an attitude towards me.

"What are you doing, I've watched you stand here for five minutes with your arms crossed; you could be sweeping under that rack," His words hit me like a ton of bricks. I felt like I was a slave and the master had spoken.

## WHAT IT TAKES TO BE THE MAN

Why should I, as a black man, be spoken to that way? I had worked hard for him; why would he address another man this way? Before I knew it, I reacted, but it wasn't in a good way.

I told him about himself and the job. He decided to walk me out of the building. I didn't care at this point. I gave him peace of mind, and I felt good about it. Slavery is over, and no man should be disrespected like that.

I had been holding shit in for too long, so as a man, I had to let him know how he and those employees made me feel. His face turned blue, and I respectfully handled him.

He wanted me to act a fool so they could say that all black men are angry and should be feared. I killed his ass with kindness. It's hard being black in a world that has a vendetta against us. We are judged no matter our backgrounds, so I stood up for what was right.

After that day, I never went back to that job. Once again, I was jobless, but at least at peace. My experience only opened up more doors, giving me the freedom to create movie scripts.

My thought was that one day, I would make a difference in this world. Coming from the bottom has a way of helping you fight for your dreams. I was elated to know that as one door closes, more will open. I decided to walk out on faith. I pray God steers my path.

WHAT IT TAKES TO BE THE MAN

# Chapter

# 10

*Trusting My Decision*

Walking away from my job affected me mentally. I wasn't sure if I had made the correct decision, but it felt right. My Dad and I conversed about it.

"Son, you don't ever leave a job unless you have one lined up,"

"I know, Dad, but they kept pushing my buttons,"

"I understand that, and that's what they do; jobs are hard to come by, especially for us black men; when I was young, I worked in the cotton fields for twenty cents a day, so when I moved up here to New York, I was satisfied,"

## WHAT IT TAKES TO BE THE MAN

"I am sorry, Dad, this is a different time; black people don't have to be just satisfied; we have more rights now, and we want to be respected,"

"I understand that, son, look. I've been at my job for over thirty years, and I have taken all kinds of shit that made me want to go off and leave, but I didn't finish school, and I don't have a diploma, so where am I going to go?"

"I understand, Dad, but that's not the position that I am in; I am a man, and I can't let people run all over me,"

"I am done letting people run over you. Just don't let them take money out of your pocket,"

"You are right, and I tried hard, and I even prayed about it, but my anger got the best of me; even though I handled my manager respectfully, I didn't curse or anything,"

"Well, I guess you did the right thing, and I don't blame you for walking out. Forget that mess,"

"That's what I said; I can't take that disrespect anymore; they monitor everything you do. Caucasians can stand around and chat during work hours, but us black men, we get written up or fired, they always watch us when we go to the bathroom, and they monitor how long we are in there,"

# WHAT IT TAKES TO BE THE MAN

"I know it's bad, son, but this is their world, and we are just in it trying to survive and stay under the radar,"

"Dad, I am tired of going under the radar; I am a man and one day. I am going to show the world it's not always about race and the color of our skin; we deserve respect also,"

"DeVon, anything that God has for you, it's for you, I don't blame you for walking out,"

"Dad, that bully Thelma was something else, and she tried to pull a Karen on me,"

"That's what they do, son, but don't let it get you down, you follow your dreams,"

"Thank you, Dad, now I have to figure out what to do next,"

"Don't worry, God has your back, and no one can stop you but you,"

"Thank you, Dad, I love you," "I love you too, son," Dad said as we ended our conversation.

I drove around the city, deep in my thoughts. I realized this was an opportunity to follow my dreams. No more obstacles were going to get in my way. After driving, I decided to go by Momma's house and chat with her.

## WHAT IT TAKES TO BE THE MAN

Momma was the total opposite of Dad. "Don't let anyone talk to you or treat you any kind of way, DeVon; you know I went through that when I was working; those bitches used to always fuck with me; and they did dirty shit; a person can only tale but so much, I believe you did the right thing,"

"That's what I told Dad, Momma. Those people were testing my manhood, and that lady Thelma I told you about, she bullied everybody except me,"

"That's why that old hag didn't like you; they hate when black men stand up for themselves; she was Caucasian, right?"

"Well, sort of; she was a German lady,"

"Same thing, they think they are better than black people, they keep forgetting we are the ones who helped built this country,"

"I can't stand disrespect; I treat everyone well no matter where they are from or what they look like. Why can't it be the same for us?"

"Unfortunately, you are a young man, judged for who you are. They believe we are all drug dealers, drug fiends, evil and angry people, but that's far from the truth,"

"There are bad people in every race, not just black people; it's just so hard for us to separate ourselves from the bad bunch no matter what we do, no matter how we talk or act, to them, we are all niggas,"

## WHAT IT TAKES TO BE THE MAN

"Until the day you die, it will always be that way, but DeVon, don't let them dim your light; God has a light on you that is so bright; you are a King, so stand in your position, pray to God and do his work,"

"I am going to do just that, Momma. I haven't told you, but I am going to college in a few weeks,"

"You are, for what?" "I want to be a movie script writer,"

"A movie script what?" "I want to write movies," "I never knew that; how long do you have to go for?" "I will go for two years, and after that, I may go back for a few more classes; I might even take some acting classes,"

"I didn't know you had that in you; you know there are writers in your family; we have some cousins who wrote books, and your Grandmother is a great writer; she writes poems for her church,"

"Wow, I didn't know that I'm not sure that I can write a book, but I can write movies and stories,"

"I don't see why not; it's the same art, just another art form,"

"I will stick to writing scripts because people love going to the movies,"

"Anything you decide to do, I have your back, sometimes; you have to walk out on faith and let God do the rest,"

# WHAT IT TAKES TO BE THE MAN

"Thank you, Momma, your support means everything,"

"That's what a Mother is for, and I will help you in any way you can; you know you may have to move out to California or New York City that's where most of the writers live,"

"I know, I have thought about it; I just can't keep working for people and getting fired,"

"Yvonne is going to love you if you get rich; she has your children, and she will be rich too,"

"Momma, now why did you say that?"

"It's true, but don't think about it, just do what's best for you son,"

"I hate to think about making her rich, but my children deserve better," I said as I walked into the kitchen to get a glass of water.

"DeVon, did you hear about your Auntie Ella?"

"No, what happened to her?"

"They let her out of that mental hospital?"

"Why did they do that? Isn't she crazy?"

"Hell yeah, she is crazy, but they said the medicine will help her; she is borderline schizophrenic,"

# WHAT IT TAKES TO BE THE MAN

"That's crazy. Do you think Ella is going to get her children back?"

"Her children don't want to stay with her crazy ass; they are almost grown anyways,"

"That's true, I hope she gets the help she needs,"

"What she needs is to stay off those drugs,"

"I don't understand why she started doing them,"

"I heard Carlton got both of them hooked on drugs and now he's off the drugs and has moved out of town,"

"He's clean, and now she's losing her mind; that's crazy,"

"I don't know how people get hooked on drugs, but she has lost her mind behind it, and now her husband is living in Boston with another woman,"

"How do you know that?" "I have my ways of finding out things," "Momma, have you talked back to your old boyfriend?"

"No, and his sorry ass better not come back around me if he know what's good for him,"

"Momma, you are still a gangster, ha, ha,"

"No, I am not, I just don't play, and besides, I am good by myself, I even started going to church,"

## WHAT IT TAKES TO BE THE MAN

"That's good, Momma, get your praise on, but first you have to stop cursing so much,"

"Boy, DeVon, shut up; no one is perfect," "I know that Momma; I was just kidding,"

"Well, it isn't funny; I know what to do now. Focus on yourself and make these children of yours proud,"

"I will, Momma; I love you," I said, and Momma smiled. Sometimes, I wonder about my Momma because she had difficulty expressing herself. I was waiting for them to tell me she loves me, but one day she will; I will ensure that.

# Chapter 11

## *A Product of Your Environment*

School started, and I was as motivated as ever. I studied and stayed home. I wasn't going to let anything distract me. That wasn't my initial thought until money got low as I waited for the school meal to kick in.

I thought about doing the only thing I once knew, and that was to sell drugs until my money came. A part of me missed that street life, but the grown man in me told me otherwise.

Why mess up everything I worked hard for? I didn't want to do that to myself. I was so close to being somebody in this world, but my

## WHAT IT TAKES TO BE THE MAN

greed for fast money stuck to me like caffeine; it was a drug, and I wanted it badly.

I didn't want to borrow money from anybody because, as a man, you are supposed to be able to support yourself. I was hungry, and I was losing weight. My pants were falling off my ass.

My Momma noticed that I was losing weight one day, and she said, "Boy, I hope you're not on crack,"

"What, no, why would you say that?" "Because your pants are sagging off your ass. Are you eating?"

"No, Momma, drugs are the farthest thing from my mind, at least taking them is,"

"What's that supposed to mean? I better not find out you are selling drugs; that's not you. I have huge hopes for you,"

"I know, Momma, but I did not have any money; I have to get it from somewhere, and the streets are all I know,"

"Those streets mean death and jail; now, if you need me, just ask, but don't you go out there and do something stupid, especially after you have come this far,"

"I know, but I was just thinking about it." "Stop thinking about it; that's not an option. God had something special for you. Just have patience. Hold up. I will be right back," Momma said as she walked upstairs. I paced around in the living room until she came back downstairs.

"Here, take this," Momma said with a paper bag full of hundreds.

"Momma, I can't take this from you," "You're not taking anything from me; I am giving it to you,"

"Momma, I can't take your life savings," "Who said this was my life savings? Besides, you are my child, and I want the best for you,"

"Momma, I can't take this," "You can, and you will; just look at it as an investment; yes, I have invested in my son,"

I smiled, and then tears fell out of my eyes. "Stop that; you are a man, you're my son, and I am only doing this because you are trying your hardest to be a good man, take care of your children, and are in school to follow your dreams. I have your back.

I took the money bag, hugged Momma tight, and said, "I love you, thank you. One day, I will make you rich women, I promise,"

"I don't care about that; all I care about is my son, doing it the right way; God will bless you; just be patient,"

"I will, Momma, I promise,
I said as I walked towards the door. I immediately turned around when Momma said those words she never says, "I love you, DeVon,"

## WHAT IT TAKES TO BE THE MAN

I stood motionless for a second, and then I went and hugged her again. "Boy, get off me, now go and pay your bills and get yourself some food; I am tired of seeing your pants slide off your skinny ass,"

I laughed, and I went out of the door. I couldn't believe Momma said she loved me too. Deep in thought, I sat in my car, and a little voice in my head said to count the money.

I couldn't believe my Momma gave me five thousand dollars. Where did she get all of this money from? I felt guilty about getting the money from her, but she wouldn't take no for an answer. I promise that one day, I will pay her back.

I headed home and stared at the brown paper bag with me in it, sitting on the passenger seat. I nearly ran the red light as I pulled a little in the crosswalk. Out of nowhere, I heard police sirens. I tried to move to the side so they could get by, but they stayed behind me.

Two Caucasian officers got out of their car, and they started yelling and cursing at me. I was confused as to what they were doing because, as far as I knew, I hadn't done anything wrong.

"Get the fuck out of the car," Officer Denton yelled.

"One false move, and I will shoot your ass, muthafucker; now put your hands on the steering wheel," Officer Spinelli yelled.

"I am; what did I do," I said, "Just put both of your hands on the steering wheel where I can see them, do you hear me?" Officer Denton

## WHAT IT TAKES TO BE THE MAN

screamed. "I am," I yelled as I stood stiff and aboard. "Get out of the fucking car now," Officer Denton yelled. "What did I do?" I yelled. "Don't move, or I will shoot your fucking ass," Officer Spinelli yelled.

At that point, I feared for my life. One tear came out of my eye, but I stood still. "Get out. Did you hear what the fuck I said? "Officer Denton screamed. "Okay, I am leaving, but what did I do?" I asked again.

"Get out now," Officer Denton screeched. I started slowly moving out of the car. I was told to turn around, put my hands behind my back, and walk backward, so I complied.

The next thing you know, I was being flipped upside down, and I landed on my shoulder. I could feel something crack. I screamed out loudly from the excruciating pain.

"Ah, what did I do?" I asked in pain. "We do the fucking asking questions around here; check his car," Officer Spinelli said.

"Ah, my shoulder, my shoulder, it hurts," I yelled as Officer Denton pushed my arms up to my mid-back area while putting those hard, steal handcuffs on me.

"Look at all this money in this paper bag," Officer Spinelli yelled.

"You must be the guy we are looking for; you robbed that bank on Remo Street; we got you now, asshole," Officer Denton said. "I didn't rob any bank; you can call my Momma," I yelled.

# WHAT IT TAKES TO BE THE MAN

"Shut the fuck up, you thief," Officer Denton yelled as he kneed me in my ribs. I couldn't breathe at this point, and I feared for my life, so I yelled, "Help, help! They are trying to kill me; I didn't steal anything," I yelled as another police car pulled up with a black female officer and her Caucasian male partner.

"Who do we have here?" Officer Johnston asked

"This is the muthafucker that robbed that bank," Officer Denton said.

"Are you sure? Because he doesn't fit the description," Officer Johnston asked.

"This is him, so let me handle my business," Officer Denton said as he yanked me off the ground and nearly broke my arm.

"Officer Denton, please calm down," Officer Johnston said calmly. "Don't you give me any orders," Officer Denton said as he shot me in the back of his car. "This is the guy," Officer Spinelli said. "Officers, please stand down," Officer Glynn said, which was Officer Johnston's partner.

"I didn't do it, I didn't do it, my Momma gave me this money, you can call her now," I yelled. "Shut the fuck up," Officer Denton said as he punched me numerous times in the right eye.

## WHAT IT TAKES TO BE THE MAN

I could barely see, and my whole life flashed before me. I have been trying to do right in life, but these officers told me I was nothing to them and the world.

"Please, call my Momma, I yelled, and Officer Denton was about to hit me again until Officer Johnston grabbed his arm and pushed him away.

Officer Denton immediately grabbed her by the arm and said, "Don't you ever fucking touch me,"

"You're going too far, sir," Officer Johnston said calmly. "You don't tell me what to fucking do," Officer Denton said as he put his hands around her neck.

Officer Glynn intervened, and it was the only thing that saved my life. They all got together, took me downtown, and even fingerprinted me. When I finally got that one phone call, my Momma and Daddy were down at the police station, raising hell.

Momma kept saying she was going to sue the police for a false arrest and for all the physical damage they did to me. I feel like less of a man because I can defend myself. Those officers made me feel shit. I was nothing to them. As far as they knew, I was just another nigga who was selling drugs.

I healed from the whole ordeal, but I wasn't the same. Those officers came close to taking my life. I stayed in the house, and I did my schoolwork. I feared for my life, and I didn't want to take a chance being amongst people, not even my family.

Months later, we found ourselves in court. The officers dropped the case against me because Momma explained that she had given me the money.

Those officers looked like a damn fool. Momma shortly filed a civil case, and we also won that case. It was a sum of $368,078.00. Months later, Officer Denton was charged with felony battery after attacking Officer Johnston.

We were so happy to hear that he was facing jail time for the whole incident. After all of that was over, I graduated from school. I learned a lot, but there was still more to do.

All my connections from the festivals never answered my emails or calls, so it was back to the drawing board. I just kept writing and trying to go to Film Festivals. No one would give me a helping hand, but I never gave up.

I sometimes wanted to give up, but I knew I was destined for greatness. Momma constantly lectured me, but I didn't want to hear what she had to say.

"You might have to move out of town, you know, go where all those movie producers are at, mostly New York or California," "Momma, I don't want to leave my children," "Why don't you take them with you?" "I wish Yvonne would have a damn fit," "Yes, you are right, she is their Mother," "She would probably kill me, but I have thought about it; maybe I will wait until they are a little older," "So, what will you do until then?" "I will keep writing, go to more festivals, and contact agents."

"What do you need the agents for?" "They will help me sell to the producers," "Well, since you don't want to leave your children, you need to get busy, don't you think?"

"I know, I am; there is a festival going to Houston, Texas, in March, I will fly down and see what happens,"

"I told you to go to New York City or California," Momma said. "I know, they aren't having there's until October of this year,"

"Both of them?" She asked. "Well, New York City is having one in December, and California's is in October,"

"Okay, now get yourself ready and write some good movie scripts," She said.

I was eager to finish my projects so I could shop for them. I went to Yvonne's house to see the children; she had a new boyfriend. He was tall and skinny and looked like he wanted to kill somebody over her.

I only wanted to see my children, but he thought I still wanted her back. This guy got pregnant with Yvonne and became even more jealous of me. I didn't pay him attention and just went to get my children.

I wasn't trying to let anyone bring me back to the streets so I could end up in jail. Yvonne's new boyfriend's demeanor was that of a street thug, and I know what those types of guys are all about.

I couldn't believe Yvonne got pregnant by a man like that, but it's her life. In the midst of that, I started taking acting classes. I kept myself busy, and I stayed in my world.

There was too much to get into in the hood, and I didn't want to hurt my dreams by indulging. The streets aren't loyal, and so far, the streets are undefeated.

# Chapter 12

## *Lost All Respect*

Now that I had all this money in my account from the case, I decided to focus on my writing craft. I spent hours daily writing movie scripts. At the same time, I was starting to have serious problems with Yvonne and her new boyfriend, J.B.

J.B.'s jealousy of me was starting to show. I would hear him in the background telling her when and where I should pick my children up, and she would echo what he said back to me.

## WHAT IT TAKES TO BE THE MAN

At times, I didn't even want to go pick them up because I knew if he said the wrong things to me, I would have to hurt him, or he would have to hurt me.

After all, she and I had been through, I couldn't believe how she would let a man like J.B. get in between our parenting of our children. Months went by with the same petty shit happening, and it got worse when Yvonne's had J.B.'s baby.

The crazy thing about him was that he would never say anything to my face; he was always behind her on the phone. I would hear his witty ass remarks while she was talking.

While Yvonne was at a doctor's appointment, he had a problem with me because I stopped by to see my children. I only stopped by for twenty minutes, and then I left.

What man would have a problem with another man seeing his children? Yvonne said something disrespectful about it. That shit pissed me off. I told her, "I will come and see my children when I want," "No, you can't just come by now. I have a man now, and I have his child," "So, what, you have two of my children," I yelled as I hung up the phone.

Yvonne called back and said, "For that, don't just show up at my house," "Yeah, that's right, don't come over here unannounced," J.B. said in the background. I heard his punk ass loud and clear. I hung up the phone and started cursing her and him aloud. The nerve of her telling me when and where I could see my children. J.B. must have her ass brainwashed or something.

As our drama intensified, I wrote a movie script about my experiences. I was happy with the plot of my new script, What It Takes To Be The Man.

I sat at my computer, emailing agents and movie producers daily. I set up my planner to attend more literary shows and Film Festivals. I wouldn't let what I was going through detour me from my blessings.

While the drama grew with J.B., I let Momma go and get my children when I wanted to see them. Yvonne and Momma got along well, so that would keep me and that fool away from each other.

Not even a full year later, Yvonne was pregnant again by that street thug. He wasn't working, but he was always out in the streets or at his family's house—at least, that's what I heard from one of Yvonne's Aunts when I saw her at the grocery store.

Right before Yvonne's second child, J.B. got arrested for murder. From what the news reporter said, he was the getaway driver and an accomplice of the crime.

J.B. was facing 25 years to life, and now Yvonne has his two children, my two children, and a little girl by the other asshole who drug her down the street in her car. I thought to myself, that's what she gets for choosing a damn loser.

Now, she had five children, all alone. Truthfully, I started losing all respect for her. I knew seeing my children now would be even more complex, which made me unhappy.

When the courts finished with J.B., they gave him fifteen years in prison. I continued to see my children, and Yvonne didn't have a problem with it. Why do women have to switch up on their children's Father when he's doing what he's supposed to do as a man? That shit baffled me.

While trying to stay consistent with writing movie scripts, I conversed with some people about how I could get my first deal. I spent lots of time on the phone trying to get through to people. I got run-around and rejections, but that wouldn't stop me from moving forward.

After all the conversations, I started feeling defeated. It wasn't as easy breaking into the business as I once thought. Momma and I had conversations about leaving the city and going to where the big film producers are kept resurfacing in my mind. Maybe that would be the best thing for me, leaving my city.

I decided to talk to my Dad about it, and he was all for it, but he asked me, "What about your children?" That question left me speechless. Yvonne was already alone and had all those children to manage. I felt selfish, but I wanted my dreams to come true.

"You know a boy needs his Dad around, so I never left your Momma when you were little. Sometimes I wanted to, but I dealt with what I had to until you were grown," Dad said.

Those words made me feel even worse. I started to rationalize with myself as I said, "I am doing this for them; if I become rich and famous, they can come to live with me,"

"That is true, but what if you don't make it? That's lost time with you and your children, and time is something you can't get back," Dad said. We conversed more about it, and I was just as confused as before he and I spoke. I didn't know what to do.

I thought the next best thing was to ask my children how they felt about me leaving them for a while, but that was the wrong thing to do. They didn't take it well and didn't want their Dad to leave. No matter how much I tried to convince them, they weren't buying it, and my daughter Imani started crying and hugging me.

I had to promise them that I wouldn't leave them and would sometimes be in and out of town to sell my movie scripts. It made them feel comfortable with what I was trying to do.

What I found out was that it's tough trying to be a Dad and follow your dreams at the same time. I didn't want to risk my relationship with my children at all. I thought of the process and figured it would be ten times harder not being in the places where I could get my scripts seen or read. How was I going to make this happen without going back on my promise to my children? What if the producers wanted me to live in the city where they were? What would I do? After second-guessing and figuring out things, I thought I would leave it in God's hands.

While in a deep discussion with myself, my phone rang, and it was an out-of-state area code. I answered the call cautiously and said, "Hello, who is this?" "I am looking for a DeVon Edwin Bell, is this him?" "Yes, this is DeVon; how may I help you?" "I have received several emails from you, are you seeking an agent for your movie scripts?" "Yes, I am, and your name is?" "I am Mitchell Freeman at Legitimate Literary Agents Inc. I see you have a movie script, is it completed?" "Yes, I have several," "I see you are Upstate," "Yes, I am," "We are located in Manhattan, New York, and I see that you are so far away; I would like to know if we can set up an appointment next month to talk about your movie scripts and what services we can help you with," "That sounds great, when is a good time?" "I will email all the dates you can come and give you some time to prepare." "So, you are going to send it to my email?" "Yes, if this email is correct," "Yes, the one I sent to you," "Several times, it looks like, so I will send you material about what we do and the dates you can come; please just confirm and let me know what dates that you are available," "Okay, I will do that, and thank you, Mr. Freeman," "Thank you, and I look forward to meeting you soon," "Goodbye," I said as a smile went across my face.

I couldn't believe the phone call I just had. All my dreams are finally coming to light. I thought as I reminisced on all the things I had been through in life. I felt good about myself, knowing that I had improved my life. It's so hard for a black man in a world that's afraid of us. I was confident that I could break all those barriers if I could share my gift with the world. I called Momma and Dad, and I told them the good news. Momma was so happy for me, and she said, "I am proud of you; you can do it; just be safe because there are people out there who will pray on your ignorance," Dad just praised me, and he said, "I am so proud of you, now you go out there in that world and show them who you are, you are gifted, and now it's your time to show everyone else,"

I felt so uplifted when I told them my good news. I must have read Mr. Freeman's email one hundred times in disbelief. I prayed every chance I got, knowing this could be my big break.

While out celebrating the great news by myself, my phone kept ringing. I tried to drink my wine alone, but my phone kept going. I finally decided to answer it because maybe someone was calling about my movie scripts.

## WHAT IT TAKES TO BE THE MAN

Just as I was about to say hello, Yvonne started screaming and yelling. I couldn't understand what she said, so I cried, "Slow down, girl, calm down; what's wrong? What happened? Is it the children?" "No, no, the children are all right; I just got a message saying that J.B. has been murdered in prison; oh my God, I don't know what to do," "Hold up, calm down, say what? Who said that?" "The prison called me and his family, someone stabbed him in there; now, what am I going to do?" How do I tell his children?" Yvonne said as she screamed and started crying.

I was in a state of shock because of how this happened. J.B. is dead, and Yvonne has all of these children. "I heard it was a brawl, and someone stabbed him seven times, can you come and watch the children this evening?"

I paused for a second because part of me wanted to say, "Hell no." But because my children were there, I had to go. I agreed to come because I started to feel bad for her, but deep down, she made her choice with a street thug, and now she needs me. It's funny how the world works.

I sat with all the children while she took care of whatever she had to; I was still in disbelief. At the same time, this man wasn't anything but trouble; truthfully, I didn't know what she saw in him.

Deep down in my gut, I knew this stupid man would do something to get himself killed. He was always looking to start trouble with me.

## WHAT IT TAKES TO BE THE MAN

Luckily, I was too strong of a real man to let a street thug draw back in.

Three hours later, when I was playing with the children, Yvonne called me and said, "I am on the way; I am leaving J.B's Mother's house now,"

"Okay, take your time. The children are okay. I am playing around with them, do you think I should feed them?"

"Yes, please. I will see you soon." "Okay," I said as I nodded my head. Yvonne put herself in a crazy situation, but I stood up and did what was right as a man. The children were never the problem; it was always their Daddy.

I still had a little love for Yvonne, or else I probably would have turned my back on her like she did with J.B. over me, but I am not that kind of man.

Yvonne had a nervous breakdown over his death, but I was always there for her. I couldn't let her give up on herself because she also had my children. I must admit it was hard seeing her caring for another man that way, but I couldn't leave her alone to take on all that pain. I guess you can say that I am a stand-up guy and compassionate, especially because she is the Mother of my children.

Life is unpredictable at times, and it's up to you to dodge all the drama and distractions that come your way. It's so difficult to survive in a world that hates to see black men trying to progress. Life was never meant to be easy and damn do I realize it, now.

My life experiences influenced my movie scripts. How could they not? I wrote and wrote. It became an addiction. The phone calls started coming in, and I was trying to pitch my movie scripts to some of the biggest producers. I was asked to schedule so many appointments that I knew I couldn't possibly keep. I pushed forward while helping Yvonne with all of the children. Now, what man does that?

As I wrote on my computer at night, an email came across. It said there would be a Film Festival coming to town next weekend. I was elated. I pulled up the promotion, and I scheduled to be there. The promotion said I could talk to some of the best movie scriptwriters.

I looked forward to bumping into some actors, authors, and producers. My time was now, and I knew I had to make the best of it. I put some of my best scripts together and made some business cards.

Finally, the weekend came, and the festival was here. It was a huge event. I walked from one end to the other, meeting writers like me. We all had the same story and were hungry for our dream to become a reality.

I ran into a beautiful woman named Amelia Davenport. Amelia was also a scriptwriter and happened to live in the city's suburbs. We conversed for a while. Our dreams and goals were similar. We

## WHAT IT TAKES TO BE THE MAN

exchanged numbers in hopes of one day helping one another if we both got that big break; after that, I passed out as many business cards as I could. I had hoped that some producer would call me.

After the festival, I went home, and the mail was at my door. I opened it, and I read what was in the envelope. "Child support papers?" What the hell is this?

The papers said Yvonne wanted to put me on child support. How could she do this to me? I have been paying her out of my pocket monthly. Maybe she wants money every week? I thought to myself. That's no problem; all she had to do was ask.

I couldn't believe it because I was there for her and at her side when she needed me. I realized you can do everything for someone you care about, but sometimes, they don't care about you as you care about them.

I knew then that Yvonne and I needed to talk because this wasn't right. I stayed up most of the night thinking about what I would say to her.

With all that was going on, something inside of me said, "DeVon keep a cool head, it has to be a reason for it," Those good thoughts overridden my evil thoughts because the other side of me wanted to curse her greedy ass out, but I was only assuming at this point. **Damn, the Devil is always busy!**

# Chapter 13

## *Let Downs And Rejections*

    I was so upset that it took me a few days to calm down before I addressed this child support with Yvonne. As far as I knew, she called those people on me. I've seen from friends and family, that child support ruins black families, especially if the Father is taking care of his responsibilities, he still ends up with the short end of the stick.

    After rationalizing with myself, I called Yvonne, and I asked her what the hell was going on and why she put me on child support.

    "What are you talking about, I didn't call child support services on you?" "Somebody had to because I have the letter right here,"

## WHAT IT TAKES TO BE THE MAN

"What letter, ok, what does it say?" "The letter states that I have to pay child support because you had government assistance at one time," "What, I only got government assistance for a short period, and that was when I had our son; this is those people wanting money from you, not me, I was only on that mess for a short time," "That's messed up because I pay you all the time," I know you do, so what do you want me to do about it?" "Nothing, never mind, these are my children, just let them take the money, and I will still give you money on the side," "Are you sure?" "Yes, they are my responsibility, don't worry, I will be okay," "All right then, because I know I hadn't called anyone, well let me go so I can take the children to the babysitters so I can go to work," "That nursing job is a good one, I see, where are you taking the children?" "Over my Aunt Lisa's house," "Okay, I will stop over there and visit them," "That's cool, but you can't take them anywhere," "What do you mean, why not?" "Because they have to watch each other," "So, I can't take my children anywhere because they have to watch each other; that's not fair to me," "Whatever, DeVon, I have to go; I have to go, I don't want to be later for work," "Whatever," I said as I hung up the phone as she was still talking.

That shit pissed me off, I can't take my children, and now I have to pay child support. Getting child support from men who are doing the right thing is a dirty system, no matter how you look at it. Black men face unfair treatment in this cold world.

## WHAT IT TAKES TO BE THE MAN

Although I had to deal with what life was throwing my way, I kept striving to do better for myself. I made call after call, trying to contact the right people in the business. I kept getting the runaround and ran into dead ends, but I wouldn't give up and quit. Some of the conversations were crazy.

"So, you have your movie script completed?" Mr. Frenchie said. "Yes, that's why I called your production, sir; I am looking to send my project to you," "I am sorry, but we don't accept unsolicited work," "Say what, my work isn't unsolicited, I am talking to you now about it," "No, sir, I mean we only take your work if you have an agent," "I don't understand that, why do I need to talk to an agent when I can just talk to you right now and send you my movie script?" "That's not how it goes; we get millions of movie scripts and don't have time to read them all." "I can understand that, but what can an agent do with my work that I can't do?" "This is a business, Sir; call back when you get an agent," Mr. Frenchie said as he hung up on me.

"That son-of-a-bitch," I said aloud. It doesn't make sense how political these film producers are. I wanted to give up, but giving up wasn't an option.

I got a call one day from an agent, and he was very disrespectful to me. "Sir, what kind of movie scripts are you writing we don't accept scripts with excessive profanity, nothing vulgar, no sex scenes, or anything of that nature; we are a respectful business, and we want our clients to be as such,"

"First of all, you don't know me and haven't even read my movie script to say what you are saying, can you tell that I am a black man because of my voice? Is that why you are saying these things to me? Are you a Christian film company or something?"

"I am only stating that we have standards and boundaries, Sir,"

"Sir, Sir, my ass, you are judging me because I am a black man and you are stereotyping me,"

"How do I know you are a black man? It doesn't matter what color or ethnic group you are, Sir,"

"Stop calling me Sir; first of all, I am Mr. DeVon Edwin Bell, and second of all, I don't need your service; I will keep looking; you have a nice day, Sir," I said as I quickly hung up the phone.

"Fucking asshole," I said under my breath. I realized this wasn't easy when getting into the business of writing and film. I only wanted to sell movie scripts to follow my dreams and take care of my family, but the obstacles in front of me became bigger and bigger along the way.

My prayers became louder and louder, but still, I felt that they were unheard. Maybe it's because I wanted things on my own. I was putting in the work with no results.

## WHAT IT TAKES TO BE THE MAN

At this point, I started preparing for the appointment with the producer in New York City for Mitchell Freeman at Legitimate Literary Agents Inc. The date was only five days away, and I started getting nervous, with butterflies in my stomach.

I worked on a presentation and looked at tutorials on how to sell my movie script. I wanted to make a good first impression, so I went to my Momma's house for encouragement.

Her words and criticism meant a lot to me. "So, Momma, what do you think about the presentation I just showed you?"

"It was good, it was good," She said in a low tone. "What, you didn't like it, any of it?" "It's not that I didn't like it; I just think you should just be yourself,"

"What, and I am not being myself?" "No, it's that people are either going to accept you or not, so why not just be yourself, it's already hard out here for a young black man to make it big amongst those people,"

"And, I understand that, but it's a game with these kinds of people,"

"You mean Caucasian people or, like we said back in my days, those prejudiced white people,"

"Yes, they have put politics in everything these days," "It's not politics; it's the color of your skin, and they judge you for that no matter if you're talented or not, so I say, just be yourself and the hell with everything else," "I see," I sighed.

"Look, son, no matter who you are or what nationality you are, if God says it's your to take, then there isn't a damn thing a Caucasian or white man can do to stop you, be yourself,":

"Okay, I got you, Momma, but why are you in this weird mood today?" I asked as she frowned and turned away from me.

"It's nothing, but your Aunt Ella is in jail,"

"Why is Ella in jail, Momma?"

"After that dumb girl got out of the hospital, they put her on meds to keep her thinking like a regular human being with some sense in her head, because you know she is crazy as hell," "What happened?" "Ellas's stupid ass got caught prostituting on Lyell Avenue,"

"Prostituting, what do you mean prostituting?" "Ellas got caught trying to sleep with a strange man for money, and she was trying to sell her stinking pussy,"

"Whoa," I said as that put me in a state of shock. "That girl is crazy; they should lock her up and throw away the key." "What did Grandmother have to say?"

"Your Grandmother and I are going to get her out of jail this afternoon," "That's crazy, well, I hope she gets some help,"

"Ella needs to stay off those damn drugs and stop sleeping with strange men, or she's going to catch a disease one day, HIV or something she can't get rid of,"

"I can't believe this, Momma; she and her family were doing good," "They were; I believe one of them did something to upset God for them to go down this bad and so fast,"

"I agree, Momma, I can't believe it, but let me get out of here; I have to take more calls and prepare for my trip; tomorrow, there's a Film festival in Buffalo, New York. I think I am going to go and bump into so many big-time executives in the film industry,"

"You do that, DeVon, and show them what you are made of; I am proud of you; I will talk to you later; now let me get dressed so I can pick up your Grandmother and get my crazy, nasty ass sister out of jail," Momma said as I walked out of the door.

Listening to Momma talk about Aunt Ella like that is very sad. Maybe God is getting back in the worst way. What she did to me will stay with me for the rest of my life. Although I never wished terrible things on her, and after all these years, I've never told her how I felt, I wouldn't wish what she and her family were going through on my worst enemy.

# WHAT IT TAKES TO BE THE MAN

I returned home and prepared my suitcase for the following day's trip to Buffalo. I started getting nervous as I packed up my laptop and ensured all my projects were on one flash drive.

After I showered, I fell asleep fast. When I woke up, I showered again and put on my clothes. I made some coffee and put all my things into my car.

I filled my car with gas at the gas station, got onto Expressway 90 West, and headed to Buffalo, New York. While on my way, Momma called me, and she sounded upset.

"Momma, what's wrong, what going on, why do you sound like you've been crying?" "That's because I have," "Why, what's going on?"

"You know when your Grandmother and I picked up Ella, she was trying to fight us," "Fight who, who is us?" "She was trying to fight mainly me, but she started talking crazy to your Grandmother and me,"

"Why, what is her problem?" "Ella got upset because I told her what she was doing was wrong, sleeping with all those men and not taking care of her children,"

"What did she say?" "She said she sleeps with who she wants to sleep with, and it's none of your Grandmothers or my business, and said we were jealous of her good pussy,"

## WHAT IT TAKES TO BE THE MAN

When I heard Momma say that, I was mad as hell, and I wanted to curse, but I held my composure. "Wait a minute, she said, what?"

"You heard me, she started talking out of her mind, so I told her she was crazy and she needed to take her meds, and that's when she started to fight me; I grabbed her hair, and she grabbed mine; I punched her in her stomach and then when your Grandmother broke us up, I punched her in her face,"

"Momma, next time, leave her in jail; I don't care what she says or does, leave her there because she has no business trying to fight you, especially after all of the things you have done for her, she's lucky I wasn't there, I would've cursed her out,"

"Ella is off her rocker; she hasn't taken her medicine because of being locked up, but she knows she can't beat me up," "What was Grandmother doing?" "After she broke us up, she started crying," "I can't believe this, Momma, please stay away from Ella; she is not the same person,"

"I know, those drugs have messed up her mind; I can't help a person who doesn't want to help themselves; well, I know you said you were on your way to Buffalo to some Film Festival; are you there yet?"

"I am almost there, but are you sure you don't want me to return home?" "No, It's okay; after I beat her ass, she was crying and talking shit; I dropped her off at her house while she was still cursing me out, "That lady is crazy, but I will call you later, once I get settled in the hotel," "Okay, don't you worry about me, I will be all right, I want you to win those producers over," "Thank you, Momma, talk to you later," "Okay, bye and good luck, I will pray for you," "Bye Momma."

When I got off the phone, I started inhaling and exhaling fast. I was mad as hell. How could she try to fight my Momma? Those emotions ran rapidly all through my body. It made me think of all of the times she molested me when I was a little boy.

I wanted to call her and give her a peace of my mind for trying to fight my Momma, but as a man, I knew I couldn't confront her. I didn't want to put my hands on her because she was a woman, but I couldn't allow her to disrespect my Momma.

My mind was clouded with negativity, but I couldn't allow it to ruin my trip or my dreams. When I settled in at the hotel, I heard all that Momma had said in the back of my mind.

I knew that the truth about what Aunt Ella did to me had to come out eventually, but I wasn't sure when.

# Chapter

# 14

## *A Decisive Conclusion*

I walked down to the hotel lobby, where so many people were. Many were there for the festival, and some were for the football game.

I sat in the lobby while people watched the football game. Many were also there for the festival. I didn't know anybody at this event, plus it was short notice, and I hadn't told anyone. That's why I was surprised when the soft hands of a woman covered my eyes from the back. I grabbed the hands gently, pulled them off my eyes, and turned around. I was surprised to see Amelia Davenport there.

## WHAT IT TAKES TO BE THE MAN

"Hello stranger, how are you, why haven't you called me?" I asked with a smile.

"Hello, the stranger is always writing; I gave you my number, and I haven't heard from you at all, but it's a surprise to see you here,"

"I guess we both can use that line; I thought about calling you several times, but I guess I just got caught up in life," I said.

"Yes, life has been kicking my butt, finances, and family issues; you know life isn't easy," Amelia sighed.

"Well, it's good to see you here," "Same to you, Mr. Bell," "Please, please, call me DeVon,"

"Okay, I shall call you by your government name," Amelia giggled. I am trying to sell my movie scripts, so I know you are here for the festival; have you had any luck lately?"

"Not really, I had a few leads, but no one wants unsolicited material, and they keep preaching how your movie script has to be perfect,"

"Amelia, I have been going through the same thing, and why do they make it so hard to fight an agent for your work?"

"And, why are they so greedy and make all the shit political, excuse my French,"

## WHAT IT TAKES TO BE THE MAN

"No, apologies are needed because I feel your pain. I almost cursed a producer out the other day; following your dream isn't as easy as I thought," I lowered my head and sighed.

"You are right, but anything that you want, you have to work hard for it," "That's true, my Momma says that to me all the time," "Then DeVon, you have a very smart Momma,"

"Ha, ha, yes, she tells me that always," I chuckled.

"Yes, shall we go to this festival and rub some shoulders?" Amelia said.

I went to my room, got my backpack, and so did she. Amelia's room was on the third floor, and mine was on the sixth floor, so we met back in the lobby after getting our things.

"Are you ready?" Amelia asked. "Yes, are you?" I asked as we headed out of the front entrance of the hotel.

We were excited and ready to network and get the most out of the festival, hopefully meeting some important people in the business. As we walked up, a man's voice echoed.

"I am Mr. George Lackalany, and I'm in the film industry; I've produced many films, today, I am going to tell you there are a few ways to sell you a movie script; one, to find a literary agent; two, show your film to potential movie companies, producers, or writers; third, you can go directly to the production companies and sell yourself and your movie script." He said all in one breath. I was very attentive, and I absorbed the knowledge like a sponge.

"Did you hear that, DeVon?" "What part?" "All of it, of course; maybe we should knock down some doors," Amelia said with a funny look. "Maybe we should prepare to go to jail," I chuckled.

"Uh ah, not like that," She giggled. "I know what you mean; that may be an option," I said sarcastically. Amelia and I went from area to area, listening, handing out business cards, and getting familiar with people and faces in the film industry.

We were both hungry, and our drive was the same. We were high-energy and very outspoken. I demanded attention, and so did Amelia. We walked around for hours and met so many people.

I was hungry, so we found a tent that sold hot food, ordered, and sat down to chat. "There are so many writers out here," Amelia said. Yes, that's why our movie scripts have to be different from everybody else's," I said as I ordered our food.

"Oh, are you paying?" "Sure, why not," I said. "You know I have money; you didn't have to do that?" "I wanted to; now stop complaining, and let's eat." "Would you like something to drink?" I asked with a smart mouth. "Since you put it that way, okay, go ahead, spend away, Mr. Man," Amelia laughed. "It's Mr. DeVon," I chuckled. "Oh no, it's Mr. DeVon, is that right?" Amelia joked.

## WHAT IT TAKES TO BE THE MAN

Amelia's energy and mine bonded immediately. The chemistry was natural, and our drive made our two paths connect. I enjoyed her company. We conversed about life as we finished our food.

Amelia and I decided to separate for a while as the evening approached. I was looking for literary agents at the festival, and she was looking for film producers. We intended to network as much as possible with different people, and we would meet back up in an hour or so.

I was addicted to all the lectures, so I went to the stage where actual literary agents told their stories and discussed the business's highs and lows.

The first literary agent I listened to was Jeffrey Coringrecker. He said he had been an agent for almost fifteen years. He had all kinds of credentials and had worked with many famous people.

"Listen, everyone, there's nothing wrong with finding an agent, we are here for you, but you can also finance your film; you don't need us; I'm not saying you don't need a literary agent literally because then I would be put out of a job; I am saying there are other options, choose what's best for you," Jeffrey said as he spoke on the microphone. I stood in silence as I listened to all the questions and answers other writers asked and took it all in as knowledge. Jeffrey was adamant about taking the bull by the horns, meaning we as writers must put the work in and not wait on anyone. I understood his message, and I planned to apply every word. I listened to a few more literary agents, passed out all of my business cards, and met back up with Amelia. We were both exhausted as we headed back to the hotel.

"I am going to my room, and I am about to pass out to sleep," Amelia said. "So am I; I have to be up early in the morning and back on the road; I have to be in New York City in three days," "Wow, you do, are you meeting anyone?" "Actually, I am meeting with a film producer, and I may try to find some agents," "Well if you do, let them know about your little friend; I have talent, too," Amelia giggled.

"I will do that and keep you in mind." "Good, and make sure you call me often, I enjoyed your company; no one in my family understands my dream of being a scriptwriter, but you do." "Believe me, most of my family is the same way; they think I'm bougie," I laughed.

"Then you know my pain?" "Yes, I do, I am just a man from a low-income family who's trying to make a change in my life," "So far, DeVon, you are doing just that; look, you could still be in bad situations if you wanted to, but you're out here trying to sell yourself and your movie script, and I applaud you," "Thank you, if you can't sleep, call me, you can always sleep in my room; there are two beds," I said with poise. "I will keep that in mind; goodnight, Mr. DeVon, and don't forget about the little people," Amelia giggled as she headed toward the elevators. "Good night, little people, my invitation stands,"

## WHAT IT TAKES TO BE THE MAN

I said with a smile. I headed to my room, and I collapsed on the bed. About two hours into my deep sleep, I heard knocks at my door. I got up with my eyes squinted and quietly said, "Who is it?" I heard a soft voice say, "It's me," "Amelia?" I asked as I opened the door.

She stood with all her belongings, a white and black blanket with a silver pillow case on her large pillow. "I couldn't sleep, so I accepted your invitation,"

"Okay, let me get my things off this other bed," I said quietly.

"Okay, thank you," She said as she lay in bed.

"Sleep well," I said. "The same to you," Amelia said as she pulled the cover over her head. Instantly, we were fast asleep. I smiled throughout the night as I could hear her softly snore. I guess we both were exhausted.

We got up early the following day, brushed our teeth, and showered. We got our things ready and went into the hotel lobby to eat breakfast before leaving. I walked Amelia to her car and hugged her tightly. "I needed that," She said. "So did I, and I enjoyed you; please don't be a stranger," "I enjoyed you also, and no, I won't be a stranger if you don't," Amelia said as she walked to her car. I opened the door for her so she could get in. "Oh, and you're gentlemen, I like that," "Of course I am; now let me know when you get home," I said as I closed her door gently. Amelia rolled down her window and said, "I will; I am going to follow you back to Rochester," "Okay, I will talk to you and see you soon," I said with a smile. "I am looking forward to it," She said as she started her car. We smiled at one another as we pulled out of the hotel's parking lot. I enjoyed her company.

As soon as I got back within the city limits, I could see Amelia get off at her exit. I kept driving the opposite way. I was all smiles until my phone rang.

"Hello, DeVon, where are you?" Momma yelled.

"I am about thirty minutes away; what's wrong, Momma?"

"Your Aunt is over here trying to fight me again?"

"Say what? Who's there with you?" "It's just me, but your Dad is on his way over here,"

"Dad, okay, well, call the police, Momma, I said. "I am. Are you coming straight here?" "Yes, I am on the way; I am tired of her trying to fight you; this has to stop. Is she huge off crack or something?"

"I don't know, but she's acting like it, but somebody more net come and get her before I kill her. DeVon, this is my house, and she's up here trying to fight me; I don't think so. I told your Grandmother I would kill her daughter," "Wow, I will be there shortly, Momma," I said as I speeded up. I was so damn upset with Ella, and after hearing her trying to fight Momma again, I knew it was time to expose her ass. I held in her secret too long, and now she dares to put her hands on my

## WHAT IT TAKES TO BE THE MAN

Momma; I knew I had to put an end to her drama, and negativity, with her smoked-out ass.

I pulled up at Momma's house and parked my car. The police and Dad were standing out there talking. I could still hear Ella in the house cursing and yelling at Momma.

The police and Dad tried to grab me, but I pulled away and walked into the front door of the house. I listened to Ella for a minute, and the words that came out of her mouth ignited my hatred for her. My heart started pumping harder, I started sweating profusely, and before you knew it, I blurted out loudly, "You molested me; let's talk about that; you touched me as a little boy; why are you talking crazy to my Momma, get the hell out of her house you molester."

When I spoke, the house stood still. The police officer didn't move; my Dad was in shock, and so was Momma. Ella shut her mouth immediately, and she walked out of the house,

"She did what to you; why didn't you tell us?" Momma said.

"I was scared you would kill her, Momma,"

"I would have if you had told us this when it happened,"

"She did what? That is nasty and crazy; I wish you had told us now," Dad said.

# WHAT IT TAKES TO BE THE MAN

"I am sorry that happened to you, but there's nothing we can do now about it," the officer said. "You should have told us," Momna said again. Ella walked out, and she didn't say a word. As we discussed some of her actions, she walked off and didn't return. I guess her guilt took over. I couldn't take her disrespecting my Momma like that.

The police finally left, and I gave Momma and Dad an ear full of what happened when I was five years old, and they were shocked and disgusted at the same time. I knew the day would come, and Ella wouldn't admit it, but I didn't care. I made sure she would never disrespect my Momma ever again, and the sad thing is that her children were there to hear it all. Now, I can only imagine how they felt. Life goes on even when people do evil things to you, so I put my head up and walked tall despite adversity.

# Chapter 15

## *Maneuvering Through Life*

The day came for me to head to New York City to talk to the movie producer, and I set up some appointments to meet with some literary agents up in Manhattan.

I drove six hours to get there, and Amelia kept me on the phone for most of the ride. She helped uplift my spirits. I didn't tell her what happened with Aunt Ella, but I told her I had family issues.

About the time I made it to the busy city, traffic was horrendous. It took an hour and a half to get across the Washington Bridge. I wish I had flown in an airplane because all that traffic made no sense. I got to the hotel around 9:30 p.m. I checked in, got my room, and went to sleep. I woke up in the wee hours of the morning, and I got all of my projects together as I prepared for my scheduled appointment with Mr. Mitchell Freeman.

The time was now, and I confidently walked into Mr. Freeman's building. The building was centered right smack down in the middle of Manhattan. As I looked out of the window, I saw skyscrapers everywhere. I sat in the lobby, seated by a secretary who phoned Mr. Freeman about me being there for our scheduled appointment.

"Mr. Bell, Mr. Freeman will see you now, so go through these doors on the left, follow the hallway with the black and white marble floors until the end, and then make a quick left into his office; do you understand those directions?"

"That's a little confusing, but I think I understand," I chuckled.

"No worries; everyone has trouble at first," the secretary giggled. Wow, you sure make it hard; it's like following the yellow brick road," I said humorously, and the secretary laughed.

I found Mr. Freeman's office without problems. He sat at his desk with some glasses on, a bald head, and a white Caucasian with long fingers wrapped around the phone he was using. He waved his hand

## WHAT IT TAKES TO BE THE MAN

for me to enter his office as he kept taking his phone. I walked in tenderly and sat in the brown leather chair before him.

As soon as he finished his phone conversation, he put all his attention on me. "How was your trip, Mr. Bell?" "It was very long," "Very long, did you drive here?" "Yes, it took me over six hours to get her and more time if you add how long I sat on the Washington Bridge in all that traffic,"

"The traffic here is atrocious, " He said with a smirk. It's so far away; I would've thought you would've taken an airplane." "I would have, but all these airplanes are crashing these days, and I didn't want to take a chance," I chuckled.

"You know there are more accidents in a car than there are in an airplane, especially here in the Big Apple," "I know that's what the say, but I wasn't taking about any chances at the moment, not to say I would never fly, it's just that right now, it's a little suspect," I said.. "I understand that; now let's get done to business, do you have your query letter?" "Query letter, what's that?"

Mr. Freeman explained what a query letter was, and I felt so depleted because I must have overlooked it. "Well, since you don't have a query letter, tell me a little about your movie scripts, or let me see a little bit of your work,"

## WHAT IT TAKES TO BE THE MAN

I pulled out my flash drive and handed it to him. "You don't have it typed up on paper?" "I mean, I do, but that would've been a lot to carry around, don't you think?" "You should always have paper form with you also; anyways, let's see what you have written,"

Mr. Freeman's demeanor told me he didn't like me. He seemed irritated, as if he was expecting something else or someone else. I couldn't tell, but my antenna went up because he criticized everything. He asked if I had a literary agent, but I didn't have one.

"I've read some of this script, and it seems too ghetto," He insulted.

"What do you mean too ghetto?"

"I don't mean for you to get offended, but this work needs to be better; it's amateur work,"

"How so?" "It has words in it that I don't understand, like I said, it's too ghetto,"

"You know what, I've poured all my heart into my work, and you sit here with a smug look, and you say my work is ghetto, Mr. Freeman, I am a product of the ghetto, and my art in writing is about where I am from; this is America, not just White America; it's Black America, Spanish America, and the list goes on; the world needs people to open up their eyes, we have a voice, and we have a life that's

## WHAT IT TAKES TO BE THE MAN

different from everyone else, I thought this was a place of diversity, but instead you are trying to keep black Americans in a box,"

"That's not what I am trying to do, Mr. Bell; you are putting words in my mouth," "I didn't put words into your mouth; they came out of your mouth with ease and with distaste; I wonder what the world would say if they found out that your establishment is racist,"

"We are not racist, and frankly, I think this appointment is over," "It was over when you saw my black skin walk into your office, but that's okay; I won't let your racist view of me stop me from reaching the top, and when I get there, I am going to spit on your shoes,"

"Do I need to get the guards to escort you,"

"No, you don't, but what you can do is get your Mother to teach some you humility; you are a damn racist asshole, no need for your guards; I am leaving anyways, white trash," I said, and I grabbed my flash drive, and I stormed out of his office.

The nerve of that prejudice muthafucka. How is my work too ghetto? He didn't even read all of my work. I believe he already had his decision about me as soon as I walked through the door. I was so irate when I left his office that I couldn't even think straight.

I called Amelia since I calmed down, and she was shocked. "Calm down, DeVon, that is only one person's opinion; do you have any other leads there in the City?" "Yes, I do. I was calm, but I didn't deserve that; I drove all this way, and he had the nerve to ask me about a query letter," "You don't have a query letter?" "No, I don't," "Don't worry, I will help you write one, but don't let this one person stop you; you have come too far now; follow your other leads, and I will work on your query letter," "Okay, I have to call my parents first, I will talk to you later, Amelia," "Okay, keep your head up," She said.

I called Momma, and I told her what happened. "I am sorry to hear that. There are prejudiced people everywhere; we can't do anything about that; your Dad is here; do you want to talk to him?" She asked. "No, I will call you back; I think I am leaving to come here tonight," "Okay, take your time, and don't give up; I feel something good is coming your way," Momma said before we hung up.

Knowing that there were people who supported me helped me to keep going. While there, I called a few literary agents to schedule an appointment, but they were all booked. I didn't let it bring my spirits down because I am not the kind of person who gives up quickly.

I returned to the hotel, showered, and then napped. When I awoke, I put all my things into my car. I bought something to snack on, filled my gas tank, and got back on the road to head home.

As I drove back, I thought of everything Mr. Freeman said. His words hurt me, but I also used his words to sink into my head so I could do better. The next time I will have my shit together. I thought there were things I could do, like write versatile movie scripts.

# WHAT IT TAKES TO BE THE MAN

Amelia is writing my query letter, so I will be fully prepared next time and not take no for an answer. I laughed at that thought. I am not trying to go to jail so that I will do things correctly.

I was heavy in thought, and suddenly, my phone rang. "Hello, who is this?" "Who is this? She is the Mother of your children," "Hey, Yvonne, what's going on? I didn't know it was you," "Sure you didn't; where are you, and why haven't you been over to see your children?"

"I am out of town, but I am on my way back home,"

"Are you still dreaming about being a film writer or or whatever you have been trying to be?"

"I am. Why is that a problem?" "Yes, it is a problem; we all know dreams only come true for some people; you've been trying for years; maybe it's not for you,"

"What are you a dream killer?" "No, I am a realist, and I say fuck those dreams and come spend time with your children,"

"Don't talk to me like that because when I was coming every weekend to get my children, you made every ese in the book for me not to see them, and by the way, no one tells me when to stop dreaming, one day you will see,"

"I will see, huh? Well, I better see you come to get these children when you get back; your children need you; your son has been getting in trouble at school; he likes fighting, just like your side of the family,"

## WHAT IT TAKES TO BE THE MAN

"You mean like your side of the family, as I said I will see them when I get home, so bye," I said harshly. "Whatever, man, you better," Yvonne said right before I hung up my damn phone.

That shit made me so upset. How could Yvonne tell me what to do when she was the main one keeping me from seeing children? Now, she feels she can talk to me anyway when I was there for her when that thug baby Father of hers was murdered in jail.

People seem to forget when you help them. One thing I won't do is let her be my dream killer; just because she doesn't have dreams doesn't mean it will stop me. I was distraught after I got off the phone with Yvonne. I almost got a speeding ticket; thinking about that conversation. I couldn't believe how she was talking to me as If I didn't want to spend time with my children when the whole time, she blocked me because of her male companions or whatever she calls them. So, people don't have any shame, and they never hold themselves accountable.

As soon as I made it home, I called Amelia. She said she would email the query letter to me, and I was so thankful for her keeping her word. I called Momma and talked to her for a while. Dad was over at her house again. I wonder what's up with that? Lately, when I call Momma, Dad is over at her house!

## WHAT IT TAKES TO BE THE MAN

I hope they are not trying to get back together. These two love each other, but they are two different people. I believe they are better friends when they aren't in a relationship, which is strange.

After conversing with her, I laid myself down and went to sleep. Two hours later, I woke up to use the bathroom and went back to sleep.

Morning came, and I woke up and prepared for the day. I showered, brushed my teeth, and got on my computer. I was shocked to see at least ten emails from literary agents.

I tried to answer them all, but I was interrupted by the sounds of a gun being shot off. I looked out the window and saw two European guys running from someone. I went outside to see what was going on.

A Caucasian male shot his gun at them. The police had made an arrest, and they were taking the guy to jail. The two men were okay but were taken off in an ambulance.

That was scary because even though I am in a good neighborhood, there is still violence. All I could think of was, what if my children were over here? Those thoughts scared me, pushing me harder to follow my dreams and get rich. I thought having lots of money and moving to a safer area would keep me and my children safe.

I called Momma, and I told her about it, and she said, "The money doesn't matter, and neither does where you live; in certain people's eyes, you are still the "N" word; you are still a black man, and this is still a racist world, there's no escaping that." I felt those words, and they resonated within my soul. Things always seem to never change..

I heard what Momma said loud and clear, but I still thought it was a chance that my children and I would be a little safer. That's just my thoughts, but I could always be wrong. This world isn't color-blind.

## Chapter 16

### *Stress is Building*

After coming from New York City, I was a little defeated. My money was getting low, and my bills were still coming, and so far, my dreams were starting to put me in debt.

I had fought so hard to get away from the streets and selling drugs. I was on the right path, but somehow, the streets are still like a magnet; they will draw you back in if you're not resilient.

I went on a drive to the old neighborhood, to the areas where my cousins and my friends hung out. I didn't think I wanted to get back into dealing, but I was curious about what the guys were doing. Everywhere I went, it was like a ghost town. I had lost contact with everyone. I decided to go to one last spot, and that was near my cousin Harold's house. They stood near the corner as if they were still teenagers. I drove by slowly, and then something told me to keep going, so I sped up. I flew past them, and I thought I heard someone calling out to me. There was no way I was going backward. I didn't care if they saw me or not, they were negative people, and I was blessed to be able to get away from all of that bullshit.

I guess I never forgave my cousin Harold for sleeping with my girlfriend Regina. Seeing him is what kept me going. All the hating shit he did to me and our relationship hit me like a ton of bricks. I wouldn't give that disloyal bum another chance to betray me and laugh about it behind my back.

I drove home, sat in front of my computer, and started writing more scripts. At the same time, I started looking for a job. I wasn't broke but didn't want to get there either. I should make money and stay out of trouble, so I put in my resume at various jobs. No, I wasn't giving up on my dreams; I was only trying to figure out another way to get into the film industry.

Sometimes, timing is everything, so I felt I should lay low and let it come to me while I did some work to realize my future. I called Amelia because it seemed like she was the only one who could help uplift my spirits.

"Hello there, DeVon; how are you?" "I am not doing too good. And you?" "What do you mean? You should be on top of the world, right?" "How I still can't sell my movie script," "Well, neither can I, but I am sure it will happen one day," "Yes, one day," "Come on now, don't sound like that, okay I have something to cheer you up,"

"What's that?" "I want you to come visit me this weekend; we can go out, have dinner, and put our heads together on writing and how to get into this crazy film business," "That sounds like a plan; what day, Friday or Saturday?" "What about both days unless you are busy?" "Am I staying in a hotel?" "Of course not, you can come stay with me," "Wow, I feel so special now," "I bet you do, so is that a yes or no?" "Of course, that's a yes; I will be there; just send me your address," I said as we conversed.

After Amelia sent me her address, I packed some of my clothes. I had butterflies in my stomach because I didn't know what to expect. I called my Dad and told him I was interested in someone, and he gave me a lecture.

"Be careful because you never know what women's motives are,"

"You are right, but she's very kind and loves writing like I do." "Oh, does she also write?" "Yes, she does," That's good, and son, I never told you how proud of you I am; you could've been in the streets doing God you know what, but instead, you are trying to make something of your life, and for that, I am proud of you, DeVon." "That's good coming from you Dad, you know you never like to express yourself," "Yes, I do, maybe, but well, I sometimes do," "Look at you, you can hardly talk and get choked up, but Dad, thank you again," "Stop teasing me, you know I love you, and I am very proud of you, now as for this woman, don't be trying to get me off the subject, you better be careful son, guard your feelings until you are sure that she is the right one,"

"But how do I do that?" "You will know in due time, but just remember to take your time." "Okay, Dad, where are you?" "I am at your Momma's house." "Again, okay, Dad, what's up with you and Momma?" "Nothing. We are just friends, and I just came over to keep her company." "I know what kind of company," I laughed.

Dad just laughed, and we hung up the phone. Momma and Dad have become well acquainted again—those two love each other no matter what. Sometimes, life shows you the truth and who really loves you. You discover what black love is all about.

The weekend came, and I headed out to Amelia's house. I was so nervous, and I guess it showed when I walked up to her door and fell against it with my things in my hand.

"DeVon, are you okay?" Amelia asked as I jumped to my feet quickly. "Yes, I am okay; I guess I missed one of the steps as I walked up,": "I hope you don't sue me because I don't have any money," Amelia giggled. "Sure, you don't. I am going to take you for every dime," I laughed. "You go right ahead, and you won't get anything but the lent from my pockets. Now come on in before I have to drag you in; I can't believe you fell up my steps," "Well, believe it, but I am all right," "Are you sure?" "I am walking, aren't I?" "Yes, you are with your smart mouth," Amelia giggled.

## WHAT IT TAKES TO BE THE MAN

We went back and forth for a while. It was funny because it seemed we had known each other for years.

"Your house is very nice," "Thank you, I've had this house for five years now," "It's very cozy," "That's how I want it to be; are you comfortable?" "Yes, I am, thank you," "Are you hungry? Do you want anything to drink?" "I am not hungry now, but what do you have to drink?" "I have orange juice, lemonade, a bottle of water, and some milk," "Some milk, I don't want any milk; I am lactose intolerant," "Crazy man, I didn't say you had to drink milk," "Ha, ha, I know I am just messing with you, water is good, thank you," I said as I chuckled.

Amelia brought back a bottle of water, and we started getting familiar with one another. I gave my life's story, and she told hers. "I can't believe you did all that in the streets; you don't seem like the quote on quote, bad guy," "That's because I am not a bad guy; I am just a man born in a poor area with poor parents, and we often have to do what we have to do to survive, " "I guess I get it, but I wasn't raised poor, we always had money, I mean my parents did, but I do respect how you've changed your life, I would've never known," "Well, that's a good thing," I said as I started walking around her house until I walked up to a room with her laptops and desktop computers were. "This is my office, come on in," "This is real nice, I love it," "It's cozy and quiet in here if you want to can set your computer up and at the desk over there," "This room is huge, two desks in it, wow," "Yes, I had this wall pushed back for more room, so go ahead and put your things in that closet," "Okay, I said as I pulled out my laptop.

"Since you are not hungry, I am going to take my shower, and if you get hungry later, we can order out, but tomorrow, we are going out to eat," Amelia said as she left me in the room setting up my laptop and flash drives.

I sat in the leather seat, turned on my computer, and checked my emails. There were a few leads and several Film festivals ahead. I lucked out when I received two emails for jobs for hire. Great interviews lined up, but I didn't want to lose sight of my dreams. Jobs can be dream killers, so I had to train my mind to know that the job would be my hustle to help my dream come true.

I started to write on my new project, but I heard Amelia singing in the shower. The water stopped, but she was still singing. I left the flash drive on my computer, went into the living room, and waited for her to come out. Since the remote control was sitting on the coffee table, I turned on the TV and searched for a good movie that we could watch. "What are you doing out here, Sir?" Amelia said as she walked out in a red robe. "I am looking for a movie for us to watch; whoa, oh, wow," I said as she stood half-naked and still wet. "What, why are you looking like that, I hope I am not showing too much," "No, no, not at all," I smiled. "Let me go and put something on before your little thing gets hard," "Hey, I don't have a little thing," "You are silly, you know what I mean," "No, I don't," I smirked. "Let me go," Amelia giggled as she went into her bedroom to put something on.

I wasn't born yesterday, but she seemed a little flirtatious, or was I imagining it? As soon as I found an action movie, Amelia came out in a short shirt showing her stomach with some booty shorts that read pressure on the back of them.

"Pressure, is that right?" I smiled. "You like my shorts?" "Oh yes, I love them." "Are you sure? I will change them if they are too much." "No, please don't do that," I chuckled.

"Okay, DeVon, I hope you can contain yourself," "I will try, ha, ha," "You are silly," Amelia said as she pulled her booty shorts down.

"I thought you were writing something in the other room,"

"I was, but I decided to find us a good movie,"

"Did you find any?" "Yes, you do like action movies, don't you?" "I sure do. That's the kind of scripts I write." "I write some of everything, but I love action films." "Maybe I can get some ideas. Is this the movie right here?" Amelia pointed at the TV. "Yes. It is, and I haven't seen it yet," "I haven't either because it just came out. Do you want some wine or anything else to drink besides water?" "Wine will be good," "Are you hungry now? I can order us a pizza," "Yes, that sounds good," "Are you saying yes to the pizza or yes to the wine?" "I am saying yes to all three," "All three, I only said two things," "I am saying yes to you too, and those booty shorts," I laughed.

"Leave my boy shorts alone, Sir; they are cute, aren't they?" Amelia said as she stood up to pull them out of her behind again. Let me call and order a pizza; what do you want?" Anything that you get is okay. "All right, now, I like my pizza loaded. "That's okay, so do I," I said as Amelia entered the kitchen to get the wine and glasses.

We drank our wine and watched the movie. The movie was perfect, but we were interrupted when the pizza man came. About that time, we were both tipsy from the wine. Amelia got our plates and some napkins, and we ate a few slices a piece.

After the pizza, we were exhausted. "Are you sure you don't want to finish the movie?" I asked. "We can finish it another time," Amelia said. "You are tired too, huh?" "Yes, it must be the wine." "It is the wine because I am feeling it." "Me too," Amelia said as she stumbled and stood up.

"Don't tell me; I have to carry you into your bedroom," I said as I stood and stumbled. Look who's talking. I saw you stumble; it might be me carrying you," Amelia said with laughter.

"Oh, you might be correct," I chuckled. I am going into my room. You can sleep in my bed, but you are not getting any." "You are funny. Okay, I will sleep on my side, and you sleep on yours," I said.

## WHAT IT TAKES TO BE THE MAN

"You say that now," She said. "Say what?" "You heard me. "Are you tempting me or teasing me?" "Neither; now, let's go to bed," Amelia said.

I followed her into the bedroom, and we both jumped into the bed. Within ten minutes, she was lying on my side of the bed. One thing led to another, and the next thing you know, we were having sex. After it was all said and done, we both stared at the ceiling, wondering what had happened while trying to catch our breath.

Her and I sleeping together wasn't planned, but it happened. "I hope you don't think differently of me tomorrow," Amelia said. "Why would I?" "Because I did not plan on that happening, I am not like that, but damn, it was good," "I didn't plan on it either, but damn, did that just happen?" "Yes, it did; now, where do we go from here?"

"I don't know," I said. "Wow, we just slept together; I can't believe it," "Neither can I; wait, what, are you saying it wasn't good?" "No, I am not saying that, but I am saying it shouldn't have happened," "Why?" "Because I should've had more control than that," Amelia said. "Don't worry about it; it was wonderful. I enjoyed it, and so did you, right?" "Of course, I did, but that doesn't make it right," "Amelia, we are grown, and it happened; let's get some sleep," "Are you sure this doesn't change the way you look at me?" "I am positive now. Good night," I said. Amelia moved closer to me, laid her head on my chest, and said, "Good night,"

# WHAT IT TAKES TO BE THE MAN

The following day, we acted as if nothing had happened that night. We hung out, went to lunch, and returned to her house. Amelia got on her computer, and I got on mine. We both stayed on our computers for a few hours before we started talking to one another.

"I am tired now," Amelia said. "So am I. Are you hungry yet?" I asked. Yes, I am. " Let's get dressed and go to dinner; it's on me," I said.

We got dressed, and we went out to dinner. The Italian food was good. We both love pasta, so we ordered shrimp and pasta. After our meal, I drove us back to Amelia's house. Amelia showered, and I did right after. We got into her bed, and she came close to me and said, "Will you make love to me? I know I was a little tipsy last night. We both were, but now, I want to know that it was real," "Yes, I understand that, and I feel the same. Amelia and I made love this time, even better than the first time. I believe this time, since it was attentional, it was better than before; this time, it meant something, and we both knew. We fell fast asleep while wrapped in each other's arms, and it felt so damn good. I was pleased as I stared at her. She fell asleep, and then I followed with a smile.

# Chapter

# 17

## *It wasn't part of the plan*

I tossed and turned until the wee hours of the morning. Amelia must have felt me moving around because she woke up. We talked about sleeping together and that it shouldn't have happened, but it did. "Did you enjoy it?" She asked. "Of course, I did." "Does this mean we are seeing one another now?" "It could be," I said, and we chuckled.

# WHAT IT TAKES TO BE THE MAN

After conversing, I dressed, showered, and put on my clothes. "I enjoyed you so much," Amelia said. "The feeling is mutual," I said as I hugged Amelia tightly.

"I have to pack up my computer," I said as I walked into the other room where the computers were. "Okay," Amelia said silently. "Amelia, did you see my flash drive?" I asked. "No, I haven't, are you sure you had it?" "Yes, I am sure, I think," I said confusingly. "Then it should be there; I didn't see it," "Amelia, I could've sworn I had it here," I said as I scratched my head. "I am sorry, I haven't seen it, I will look for it when you leave, and I will call you if I find it," "Okay, yeah, maybe I left it at home and thought I brought it," I said as I second-guessed myself.

I got my things and left Amelia's house with an uneasy feeling. All the way home, I kept reaching for my computer bag to see if my flash drive was in there. I made it all the way home, and still, I hadn't received a call from Amelia. I could've sworn; I had that flash drive on my computer. When I got home, I continued to search but found nothing. Luckily, I had a backup and only had one project on it because it was a new drive.

Before I could relax in my house, the phone rang, and it was Yvonne. I could hear her cursing, yelling at me, and asking me when I was coming to get the children. "I can come to get them now," I said, "No, you can't, now, is not a good time; I have to go to work," "What does that mean, I can still come get them," "No, I want to be there when you come and get them," "Why?" "Because I said so," Yvonne said. I was frustrated, so I agreed to do whatever she said. It's like I couldn't win with her. Why fight? I would instead give up, but I would never give up on my children, only communicating with a manipulator like Yvonne because I felt like I didn't have any choice.

As soon as I got off the phone, I started looking for my flash drive. I still couldn't find it, so I started reflecting. Where could it be? Then, a thought crossed my mind, and it wasn't good. I wonder if Amelia stole it? But, Why? It could be, I thought. I had no proof, so I put it out of my mind. I went to the computer store, bought a new one, and transferred my movie script.

After that, I printed some copyright papers and filled out the paperwork. I printed out my movie script, put it in a large yellow envelope, and went straight to the post office.

I hurried back home and sat there in silence. I had to protect myself if my movie script was in the wrong hands. I headed over to Momma's house after sitting for a while, deep in thought. I couldn't create anything because I wondered if Amelia had stolen my movie script.

When I got to Momma's house, Dad's car was in the driveway. I shook my head because those two knew they still loved each other. As

# WHAT IT TAKES TO BE THE MAN

I exited my car, my cousin Harold drove up. I tried to act like I didn't see him, but he called out my name.

"DeVon, hey cousin, can I talk to you briefly?" Harold said. "I am in a hurry," I snapped. "Hey, DeVon, oh hey Harold, I haven't seen you in a while," Momma said as she walked out onto the porch. "Hello, big cousin, yes, I know, I have been busy," Harold said. "Busy, huh, too busy to come to see your big cousin?" Momma said. "You know how it is," "Yes, I do; all excuses, just like your cousin DeVon here, are you coming in?" Momma asked. "No, I just want to talk to DeVon for a minute, but I will come back to visit," Harold said. "Okay, let me get back in this house; I was watching a movie with your Dad, DeVon," Momma said as she walked back into the house. "Are those two getting back together?" Harold asked. I shook my head and said, "Those two still love each other, I don't know, so what's up?" "I just want to apologize for what I did to you with Regina; it's been weighing on my mind," "That was a long time ago; I am not worrying about that anymore," "I know it was a long time and I should've apologized, I was just thinking how I miss having you around," "We did have fun, but things happen," "Yeah, I fucked up, and I know I did, I should've never done that to you, I am sorry, and I hope you forgive me.

I was thrown back as he kept saying he was sorry for what he had done in the past. A part of me wanted to tell him to get the hell on, but I had matured, so I accepted his apology, and we talked about old

# WHAT IT TAKES TO BE THE MAN

times for nearly an hour. Although I accepted his apology, I would never forget what he did, and I told him that. We both accepted it for what it was. We hugged, and Harold left. I felt better, but I knew I could never trust his ass again. I walked into Momma's house, and Dad stared me down as if he knew what Harold and I were discussing.

"Are you okay, son?" "I am okay," "Are you and Harold okay now?" "What do you mean? Why do you ask that?" "I overheard you two and what you were talking about," "You were eavesdropping, Dad?" "No, but listen, I went through the same thing with your cousin Demetrius; he slept with one of my old girlfriends behind my back," With who, Momma?" "Hell no, boy, it was before she and I were talking; the girl's name was Betty, but anyways, I've been through something, and that's why I stopped hanging with all of my friends; you can't bring any women around them because they will get your girl," "oh, I know, and it hurts," "I have been there, but I won't tell your Momma about it," "Thanks Dad, I appreciate that," "You are okay though, right?" "Of course, that was a long time ago," I said, "what was a long time ago?" Momma asked, and Dad and I stayed silent as we walked into the house. We instantly changed the subject as Momma kept trying to get into our conversation. "Please, let's watch the movie," Dad said. "Hey, this is my house," Momma said, and we laughed.

The movie was good, and after that, Momma asked Dad to go to the store for a few things. "I heard about this new girl you are talking to," She said. "What, Dad can't hold water, can he?" I said. I told Momma all about Amelia, and she gave me the same advice Dad gave me.

"You be careful with that woman; these days, you just can't trust them, and that's coming from another woman," Momma said. Those words made me think about the time when Momma cheated on Dad with that man. I wouldn't dare bring that up, so I kept it to myself, but I listened to her advice anyway.

"DeVon, did you know Ella's husband Carlton moved out of the state with another woman?" "Wow, he did; she hasn't been back over trying to fight you, have you?" "No, she came by two days ago, and she was cordial but still crazy because she was talking to herself; I just stared at that crazy slut," "Don't forget that's your sister," "I know but she's still a crazy slut," "Her husband left her and the children, huh?" "The crazy thing about it, I heard he's the one who got her hooked-on drugs, and now he doesn't do drugs anymore," "I wonder how does she feel?" "Feel, feel, when you're on drugs like that, you don't feel," "That is shocking," I said as Dad walked back into the house with two bags of food and drinks.

"I have to go; I have to go and write." "You go ahead, one day, someone will buy your movie script," Dad said. "Don't forget to remember what I said about that girl," Momma said as she pointed at me. I looked at Dad, and he put his head down as if he had not told Momma a thing. I smirked and walked out of the house.

While on my way home, I decided to stop at the store to get some chips. As I walked out, I ran into no one other than my ex-girlfriend Regina. I was flabbergasted because I had talked to my cousin Harold a few hours ago. Regina looked different, and she seemed distraught. "Hello, DeVon, it's nice seeing you again." "Wow, yes, this is a surprise, how are you doing?" "Have you been taking care of yourself?" "Truthfully, can you hold on a second, let me get some juice out of the cooler first; I need to talk to you," "Okay, I said as I stood near the cashier in front of the store. I thought, I wouldn't give this woman the time of day, but she wasn't looking like herself, and I could tell she needed someone to talk to.

"Thank you for waiting; if I were you, I wouldn't want to talk to me anymore, especially because of what I did to you,"

"That was a long time ago, I am okay now, it's funny because Harold came by to see me today,"

"He did?" "Yes, he did," "I haven't seen him in years either, especially how he treated me, but I guess it was well deserved because of the way I did you, and karma will get you," "Yes, it will, but I am over it,"

# WHAT IT TAKES TO BE THE MAN

"DeVon, you were my best boyfriend, and I messed that up. I am woman enough to admit that; I want to apologize because I should never have slept with your cousin; because that brought a wedge in between you guys and you are family,"

"Yes, it did, but it's water under the bridge, are you okay?" I asked as Regina started coughing. "Please walk me to my car," Regina whispered.

"It's right here. To answer your question, no, I am not all right, I found out I have HIV, and I am taking medicine,"

"You have what, when, how?" "It's a long story, but every day I pray that this is a bad dream, but my reality is I am suffering from this disease that is inside of me; I don't know if I will wake up the next morning," Tears rolled down her face. I was shocked to hear what she was telling me. "Did it come from my cousin Harold?" "Oh no, we had stopped talking many years before this, my boyfriend Terry Barkett, I found out he was fucking those prostitutes, and he gave me this shit, and now I don't know if I am going to live or die,"

"Where is he?" I asked. "He's dead, somebody killed his nasty ass," She said. I wanted to ask her if she had anything to do with him being dead, but I couldn't get the nerves up to ask.

"I am sorry you are going through this, but there are medicines out here to keep you alive, you know that, right?"

## WHAT IT TAKES TO BE THE MAN

"I know, I am in the beginning stages of taking some, but this is scary," "I bet it is; does your family know?" "My parents do, I let them down so much, and at night, all I can do is cry,"

"Regina, listen, what happened with us was the past; I would never want to see anyone go through something like this alone, keep your head up and do what the doctors say, and I believe you can live a healthy life,"

"You always knew the right things to say, but enough of me telling you my lows; it was good to see you, and you look good; again, I just want to apologize,"

"Your apology is accepted; make sure you take the medicines the doctors give you; I will pray for you; take care,"

"Thank you, DeVon, I will, and please pray for me." "I will pray for you, Regina, oh, and give me your phone number; I would like to hear more about your story," "It's really not that exciting," "You never know, it might help somebody one day," "I doubt that, but I will give you my number," Regina said as she gave me her number and walked off. I could hear her coughing; I could only feel sorry for her. Even though she had done me dirty in the past, I still showed compassion. It was hard to see her in that state of mind and health. I couldn't believe it. Life has a harsh way of putting you back in your place; it will humble you.

## WHAT IT TAKES TO BE THE MAN

Running into Regina made me look at life differently. Now, I had to put things in perspective. The energy you put in the world might come back to haunt you. Without being bitter, I still pray she will be okay and live a long life.

I arrived home, showered, and got on my computer. Sitting there, I started jotting down some of what Regina told me. I realized her story was a powerful one, so I started writing a script called "Down the Rabbit Hole,"

Her story reminded me of that because sometimes you go to a place where you know you shouldn't be going, but your curiosity takes you there, and once you're there, there may not be any returning. Regina made a choice that led her down a rabbit hole, and now, she's trying to find her way out. At the time, it made sense to me, so I started writing late at night.

Just as I was about to go to bed, Amelia called me, and we talked for a couple more hours. For some reason, Amelia seemed dull, so I hurried up and got off the phone with her. Maybe she was just tired, I thought. I fell asleep for three hours and was right back up typing on my laptop.

Before going back to sleep, I read a couple of emails. Two literary agents reached out, and one of them, Matthew Granite, left his phone number.

# WHAT IT TAKES TO BE THE MAN

I was a little hyped but not overly excited. I couldn't wait to see what the next day had in store for me. I got back into bed and fell asleep.

WHAT IT TAKES TO BE THE MAN

# Chapter

# 18

*Trying To Find My way*

The following day, I woke up, sat back at my computer, and wrote down some ideas. Afterward, I made myself a cup of coffee and received a phone call about a job interview.

It had been a while since I worked, and I needed cash to make my dream a reality. I set up the interview for the end of the week. I hated working for other people, but sometimes you have to do what you must do, and right now, my dream depends on it.

After I had eaten, Matthew Granite emailed me. I immediately called the number that was left in the email.

"Hello, is this Mr. Matthew Granite?" "Yes, it is, who do I have the pleasure of speaking with?" "This is DeVon Edwin Bell, the one you emailed," "Oh yes, the screenwriter, it's a pleasure to get in touch with you finally; a colleague of mine had your business card; they said they met you at a Film Festival, so I just wanted to get some insight on what you were trying to do with your project,"

"I need someone to represent me; I need someone to talk to these big film companies on my behalf to read my scripts since they won't accept unsolicited material and someone who has my best interest at heart."

"I understand that, and I will help you as much as possible; now, where are you located?" "I am located in Upstate New York,"

"Bummer, I am in Los Angeles, California." "Wow," "Yes, would you like to fly out in a few weeks and meet me and some film producers out here?" "Of course it's possible," "I know it is asking a lot, but can you send me some of your script to read first, I am getting ahead of myself, and if I feel I can represent you, I will let you," "Yes, sure, I will send it right now," "Okay, I will get back to you before the end of the day," Matthew Granite said as we hung up.

All I could think about was him asking me to fly to California. That was a scary thought, but I knew if I was going to have some success in screenwriting, I needed to leave home and chase my dreams.

The excitement overwhelmed me, but I was brought back down to earth when I got a phone call from Yvonne. "You can come get your

# WHAT IT TAKES TO BE THE MAN

children today," "Okay, what time?" "Anytime today because I have an appointment later," "Okay, I will be there in an hour,"

Even though I hated to hear her voice sometimes, it was good to know I could finally spend time with my children. I was paying all that child support and still couldn't see them when I wanted to; the law wasn't right. I started getting dressed to go and pick up my children, and then I got another phone call, and it was Momma.

"DeVon, have you seen your cousin Harold?"

"Not since the day he came to your house, why?"

"His Mother called me today, and she said he is missing,"

"Missing, how can a grown man be missing?"

Well, Vanessa said she and Harold had an argument, and he stormed out of the house without his wallet with his ID in it, and she hadn't seen him since,"

"Maybe he's over a girlfriend's house or something,"

"Maybe, but why would he leave his wallet?"

"That's a good question," I said. "Look out for Harold, and if you talk to him, let him know his Mother, Vanessa, is looking for him,"

"I will let you know if I hear from him, but most likely, he's probably with some girl," "He probably is with some little slut,"

## WHAT IT TAKES TO BE THE MAN

Momma said. I hung up with her, but part of me was worried because it was not like Harold to disappear without his wallet and ID.

After talking to Momma, I was getting a little concerned because Harold was still missing. Family members were reaching out to me, some of whom I had not heard from for years. This was serious.

My mind was clouded with what-ifs and what happened. I also thought about how Harold came to me after all these years and apologized.

I had to clear my head before picking up my children, so I drove around the neighborhood several times. I was so delighted to see my children, and they were glad to see me. I almost cried when they hugged me so tight.

Yvonne just stood at the door with a look of disgust on her face. I don't understand that woman. Why does she hate me so much? Anyway, I blocked her negativity out as my children got into my car.

"Bring them back tonight," Yvonne yelled. I stared her up and down, and I pulled off. The things I wanted to say, I wouldn't because I didn't want to disrespect my children's Mother in front of them. I was too much of a man to do that. I knew that one day, her karma would be coming her way, too. I decided to let God handle it. I just enjoyed my children. We ate, we laughed, and we had so much fun. They made my life complete no matter what I was going through. I thanked God for them. On my way to take them back home, Yvonne must have called me at least twenty times to see when I was bringing them back home; I just ignored her.

When I arrived at Yvonne's house, she was waiting on the porch., in the door, like she was some damn warden at a prison or something. I hurried and dropped them off. Yvonne stood in the doorway, rolling her eyes, and while I was pulling off, I heard her yell out, "You could have answered the damn phone," I blocked her out as I could hear my children say, "Bye, Daddy, we love you," That's all I needed to hear.

On my way home, I received a phone call from Matthew. He said he loved my movie script and wanted to meet me. He even suggested that my fare would be paid for; all I had to pay for was my food. I was so excited.

I always daydreamed about my dreams becoming a reality. Although Matthew told me this was only the beginning, we had lots of work. We had to prepare to get Producers to like my work and accept it.

All I could think about when he and I got off the phone was that I could take care of my children and maybe take Yvonne's ass to court and take my children from her, but my good heart couldn't think about taking children from their Mother. Yvonne's hatred for me for no reason made me feel this way, but regardless, I knew that once my movie scripts were purchased, things would change for the better in my life, and Yvonne would respect me.

I was all in my feelings as I started thinking about everything I was going through. My struggles as a man were beginning to get to me and challenge my sanity. Everywhere I turned, there was a battle to fight, and all I wondered was when I would see victory.

When I arrived home, Momma called me again and asked if I had seen Harold. I couldn't believe that Harold hadn't been found yet, and this was out of character for him. Where could he be?"

The police were notified of a missing person and said they would be on high alert for him if he turned up. My cousin Vanessa kept calling me because she knew how close Harold and I once were. I wish I could tell her something good, but I didn't know where to start as far as to locate him.

My phone rang off the hook for hours, and even the police called and asked me questions. I don't know how they got my number, but they were inquisitive. I told them what I told everyone else: I don't know Harold's whereabouts. I turned off the ringer on my phone and laid in bed while staring at the ceiling, wondering where in the hell could Harold be.

# WHAT IT TAKES TO BE THE MAN

I fell asleep for an hour or so, and then I turned on my phone's ringer. It immediately rang. It was Amelia. I told her what was happening, and she sensed I was distressed.

"I am sorry to hear about your cousin; if you want someone to talk to, you can always come out here to my house if you need to get away," "Thank you, I will come to see you tomorrow, and I appreciate you, Amelia," "Sure, anytime; that's what friends are for; we are friends, aren't we?" "Of course, and more," "Thank you, I needed to hear that," Amelia said as we hung up the phone.

I fell asleep, and I woke up early the following day. My phone was still ringing. Harold hadn't shown up, and my family was getting together to try to find him. We met at an undersized center that had a capacity of one hundred people. It's funny because many of my family live in the same city as me and we haven't seen each other for years. I guess that's sad, but it seems as if all black families live that way. The only time we get together is if something bad happens or a death in the family.

My cousin Vanessa put Harold's pictures on the show Missing People. We got together as a family, and we prayed. I had a big family, but you would never know that because half of them don't get along, and some think they are better because they are financially set in life. That's how black families are; there is so much jealousy and for no reason at all. Besides all the bad things, when there's a death in the

## WHAT IT TAKES TO BE THE MAN

family, we come together, and love spreads. Some family members exchanged phone numbers, and we vowed to find our cousin Harold.

It was good seeing everyone together, but I had to go. Luckily, I had some extra clothes in my car. I called Amelia and told her I was coming to her house.

Just as I reached Amelia's house, she was pulling up simultaneously. "You made it here just as I pulled up," "Yes, I see that; this has been a draining day," "I believe you, I want to hear about it later, but I need to get to the grocery store to get something tonight for dinner; I haven't had time to shop; would you like a steak, broccoli, and candy yams?" Yes, that sounds good," "Well, here, take my key, and you can stay here until I come back; I shouldn't be long," Amelia said as she handed me the key.

"I will be right back," Amelia said as she backed out of the driveway. I opened the door, and I took my things inside. I sat on the sofa and thought about everything that had happened that day. It was so emotional, and I hated seeing my family in pain like that, especially my cousin Vanessa; Harold was her only son out of three children. I can't imagine the pain she is feeling, and the guilt must be killing her inside.

I still don't know why Harold was arguing with his Mother in the first place. That must have been a very heated conversation. I sat there on the sofa while rubbing my head. Amelia came back home about forty-five minutes later, and I still hadn't moved. I was stressed the hell out. The first thing she started doing was massaging my neck and my temples. It felt relaxing.

"Let me take these bags into the kitchen, you sit, or you can lay right here until I am finished cooking; it shouldn't take long,"

"Thank you." "No, no need to thank me; that's what friends are for, after you eat and shower, I will finish massaging you; you have so much tension built up," Amelia said.

I enjoyed her attentiveness because these past days have been hectic as hell. I was so glad when dinner was done. We sat at the table and said our prayers. The food was delicious, and just as promised, Amelia took care of my tension afterward.

I got out of the shower and lay in her bed. She brought out some massaging oil and rubbed me down nicely. I told her everything that was happening to me, and she sympathized.

"Did I tell you about the literary agent that wants to meet me in California," I said in a low tone. "No, you didn't, is he any good?" "From what I researched, he is," "That's good, make sure you let him know about me and my work," "I will make sure if he's my agent, he will be yours too," "That's sweet," Amelia whispered. After I was relaxed, we started kissing and having sex. It was much needed.

## Chapter

# 19

*Taking What Life Throws At You*

When I woke up the following day, I could smell breakfast being cooked. I looked over at Amelia's side of the bed, and there was a note saying, "Meet me downstairs for breakfast." I smiled, jumped up, went to the bathroom to brush my teeth, and washed my face.

"Good morning, good morning, I got your note; that was sweet," "I thought I would leave you a note because I didn't want to bother you while you slept," "I do appreciate it, but how long have you been up?"

"About an hour now, here, would you like some coffee?"

"Yes, sure, wow, look at you, I smelled bacon, I saw eggs and some fruit, is this for me?" "Yes, it's for you, well, us; I see what you've been going through, and I just want to be here for you,"

"It's been rough lately, so I do appreciate it," "Good, now sit on and drink your coffee, and let's eat," "Yes, I am hungry," I said as I sipped my coffee.

"Did you bring your computer?" "No, I was in a hurry, plus I had just left my family." "Okay, I see, well, let's eat, and we can talk later." "Okay, Boss Lady," "Stop calling me that," Amelia giggled.

"What?" I laughed as I put my hands up in the air. Amelia fixed our plates, and we ate in silence. As soon as I finished my plate, she put it in the dishwasher. I washed my hands in the bathroom sink and sat on the sofa.

## WHAT IT TAKES TO BE THE MAN

"Are you full?" "Yes, I am very; the food was delicious; I didn't know you were a chef," "There are many things you don't know about me," "That's fair, but I would like to know," I smiled.

"The same here, can we get serious for a second?"

"Yes, sure, what's going on?"

"I would like to know where we stand, are we a couple or what?"

"Whoa, wow, are we a couple?" "Yes, are you scared of a commitment?" "I am not scared of a commitment; it's just we never talked about it," "I know, and that's because I found myself in bed with you too fast," "I wouldn't say too fast, I like you a lot," "But, not enough to be my king?" "I didn't say that; we can work that out if you want to," "I like you a lot, and I appreciate you, and honestly, I don't want to be your fuck buddy; I want something of substance," "Wow, I didn't know you felt that way," "I just told you there's a lot you don't know about me," "I guess not," "So, so?" "So what?" "Are you even listening to me, DeVon, are we in a relationship or not?" "Let me think about this," "What is there to think about, you didn't say that when you were having sex with me last night,"

"Whoa, come on now, you just throw this line of questioning on me, I didn't say no, but I do need a second to digest everything, I like you and respect you a lot; I want to make sure I can be the man to make you happy,"

"I don't have to think about it because I know what I want; maybe it was a wrong idea to invite you here," "No, it wasn't; I enjoyed you, I am not telling you no; just let me think, and we will discuss this again soon, I have an appointment in three hours, so I have to go," "Just go, DeVon, you don't have to give me an answer,"

"Stop it, I want to give you a correct answer; now I have to hit the road, I will call you when I am finished," I said as I got my things together. I went to hug Amelia, and she shrugged me off.

I didn't mean to hurt her. I thought I was doing the right thing by giving myself time to digest this conversation. I was caught off guard. My mind was full of thoughts as I drove home. I could tell Amelia was very upset. I hated to leave her that way. I hope she's not done with us. I need some time to think it all out. I guess I was having self-reservations because I felt Amelia had stolen my flash drive from my computer. I didn't have proof, but I was willing to forget about it, but it was eating at me. I was shocked when she asked if we were in a relationship out of the clear, blue sky. It made me wonder if she had a motive or not.

When I arrived home, I dressed for my interview for the new job. I was a little behind in time, so I rushed. I managed to make it to the interview just in time. I must admit that I was a little upset that a young Caucasian young man was interviewing me. I could tell he was younger than me because of the way he talked and looked. It made me

## WHAT IT TAKES TO BE THE MAN

wonder how he got this position when it's so hard for me to stay working at one job over the years.

It made me realize how hard this world is for black men like me and that we have to work twice as hard to get into positions where we are a boss or someone who can hire others.

The interview went well, but I did have some reservations about the place because I only saw three or five black people out of two hundred Caucasian men and women. I don't know how this is supposed to be equal opportunity for black folks.

I walked out with my head up because I knew I would not need their job one day, primarily when the job was only meant for their race. Seeing this made me want to work harder for my dreams. My California trip was ahead of me, and I knew I had to make the best of it. I headed to my Momma's house after that. There were about five cars outside of her house. I got out of my car and walked up to the door, and it was open, so I walked in.

"What's going on?" I asked. Ella, my cousin Vanessa, my Grandmother, and Harold's younger brother Luke were there. "DeVon, there is still no word from Harold, and Vanessa is pulling her hair out and stressing over there." "Have you heard anything?" Momma asked as my cousin Luke stared me down.

# WHAT IT TAKES TO BE THE MAN

"I haven't heard anything or seen him," I said. "Hey, big cousin," Luke said as he hugged me. "I am so sorry, little cousin, I wish I knew where he was at," I said. "We all do, man. I miss my brother," Luke cried. Then Vanessa started crying, and shortly after, everyone started screaming and trying to hold back tears.

Momma, Luke, and Ella went to hug Vanessa while I walked outside to get some air. I kept wiping my tears off my face. I wanted to cry, but a part of me remembered what he did to me with Regina. He ruined our relationship years ago, and whether he's family or not, should I even care? Those were the words in my head talking to me, but again, I still had compassion, no matter how dirty he did me.

As I stood out on the porch, Ella came outside. "Are you all right, I know how close you and Harold were," I nodded in silence. I had to take a second and look at Ella. Her clothes were dirty, her hair was messy with off-white and black dreads in the hair, and her lips looked burnt from smoking that glass pipe of crack. Before I answered Ella, she started talking to herself while I was sitting on the porch by myself, "This muthafucka is crazy," They say mental health runs in every family. I believe she is suffering from that, or those drugs she had taken fucked her mind up.

"DeVon, I am sorry if I did anything wrong to you when you were a boy, I don't remember, but if I did, I am sorry," Ella said. I couldn't do anything but sigh. I was shocked that she said something about it.

## WHAT IT TAKES TO BE THE MAN

"Don't worry about it," I said with a rough tone. "No, I don't remember, but I hope I didn't cause you too much pain," Again, I looked at her with a shocked expression. Deep down in my heart, I felt she remembered; she was using the excuse of what those drugs did to part of her mind. If any grown person touches a child in that way, they know what the hell they are doing. I nodded my head once again, and then flashbacks of what she did to me ran through my mind. I thought about all those times I couldn't get my dick up after she molested me. It all came to me; the reason why I couldn't get it up was because I was getting touched at a much too early age, and maybe she had an infection or something, and it messed up my system. I started getting irate while she talked, so I walked back inside. Vanessa and Luke hugged me as they were about to leave. My cousin Vanessa was adamant about trying to find her son Harold. I hugged the two of them before they walked out to their cars.

"Hold up, Vanessa. I am coming with you. Can you drop me off on Lyndhurst and North Street?" Ella said.

"Ella, don't you go over there and buy those drugs?" Momma said. "I know; I am not," Ella said with a frown. You could tell she was lying. Momma and I gave each other a funny look as they pulled off. He blew his horn, and I waved.

Dad pulled up as they left, and we filled him in with everything. I walked into the kitchen while in deep thought about how Ella was

## WHAT IT TAKES TO BE THE MAN

acting as if she didn't remember molesting me. It was hard to keep my composure. I cursed out loud and walked back into the living room where Momma and Dad were sitting.

"Are you all right, son?" Dad asked. "Was that you in there yelling something?" Momma asked. "I was talking to myself," I said. "Dad laughed. "Keep talking to yourself, and you will be in the same boat as your Aunt Ella," Momma said. "Yes, crazy as hell," I chuckled.

"I am all right; I am just a little frustrated," I said. "We all are?" Momma said. "I saw Vanessa pull off; they still haven't found Harold?" Dad asked. "Nope, he still hasn't shown up," I said. "And Vanessa is losing her mind; I sure hope she finds that boy," Momma said. "I can't imagine what she's going through; I would be going crazy if I lost you, son, Dad said. "That's crazy because he had just come by here, remember?" I said. Momma and Dad nodded their heads. It's scary how your life can change in a matter of seconds.

Suddenly, there was a knock at Momma's front door. "Who is it, come on in; the door is opened," Momma said. "Hello, everyone," my cousin Big Henny said as he entered the house. "Hey, Henny, it's been a long time," Dad said. "Boy, what have you been eating?" Momma asked. "Cousin, I have been eating everything," Big Henny noted, and we laughed. "DeVon, I need to talk to you for a second, can we go outside?" Henny asked. "Yes, sure, it's good to see you; we haven't

# WHAT IT TAKES TO BE THE MAN

seen each other in a long time," I said. "It's been a few years, but I am still in the same place; I just work a lot, and I heard you have been out here doing bad things with yourself," "I am trying to get into the movies," "I hear, and there ain't anything wrong with that, especially knowing from where we come from, I am proud of you," "Thanks, so what's going on, Henny?"

"I didn't want to say this in your parents, but the word on the streets is that someone killed Harold and buried him in one of the backyards off Lewis Street," "What, who said that shit?" I asked with anger. "I heard the talk, and I am not sure it's true because you know Harold was a good fighter," "I know, the only way they could get him like that was if it were a lot of them or they had guns," "That's the other thing, I heard he was shot in the head, and that's how they got him," "That's crazy," I said as tears fell out of my eyes. "We are going to find out who did this," Big Henny said. "Yes, they can't get away with this," I said. "I will keep you posted if I hear anything else," Big Henny said as he got into his car and pulled off.

Hearing that someone may have taken Harold's life hurt my heart. As I said, the streets have a way of dragging you back in. I want to get whoever did this to my cousin, is my first thought, but then I think how far God has taken me away from the streets, and it keeps my mind in turmoil because I genuinely want revenge. Look, I am only human!

## WHAT IT TAKES TO BE THE MAN

I walked back into the house, and Momma and Dad asked me what Big Henny and I discussed. At first, I didn't want to tell them, but I couldn't keep it quiet. "Whatever you do, don't tell your cousin Vanessa that," Momma said. "That might kill her, and don't you go out in the streets trying to get yourself caught up in that street mess," Dad said. "But, he was my cousin, Dad," "I understand that, but sometimes, you have to let God take care of that; you have come too far in your life; I'm proud of you son and your Momma is too, we don't want to see you in trouble or jail, son," Dad said. My eyes teared up. I knew what Dad said was right, but it hurt to know someone did this to Harold.

"DeVon, listen to you Dad, God made you special, and you will go out there and do big things for yourself, Let God handle this battle; he will get the greatest revenge, so stay out of it and keep following your dreams," Momma said. "Soon, you will be a star, or have you star in Hollywood," Dad said. "I don't know about that, Dad, but since you brought it up, I am flying out to California to meet another literary agent," I said. "See, God already has your path, so don't mess it up," Momma said. "Listen to your Momma, DeVon," Dad said. I nodded and prayed, then took a deep breath as I sat on the sofa. "I know, son, it will be all right," Dad said. "It will be okay, son," Momma said.

We sat silently for a moment, and then I told them about my trip and future endeavors. Momma and Dad were curious about everything happening with me, so I finally told them about Amelia. "I want to meet this woman," Momma said. "Why are you keeping her a secret? I hope she's not crazy like Yvonne," Dad laughed. "No, she's not like that; I mean, I don't think," I said. "You let me be the judge of that; you know your Momma will know as soon as she walks in the door," Momma said. "I know," I said. "Let us meet her," Dad said. I sighed, and then I said, "All right,"

I wasn't sure how this would go because Amelia was upset with me when I left her house. I don't know if she is still speaking to me. I knew if I was going to decide to be with her, she would meet my parents. I didn't need their approval; I just hoped they would like her. I guess you could say I wanted some reassurance.

# Chapter

# 20

## *Make It All Make Sense*

I went home that evening, a very shaken man. There were still no clues as to where Harold was, and I knew I had to call Amelia and see where her head was.

# WHAT IT TAKES TO BE THE MAN

"Hello, Amelia, how are you doing?" I asked. There was no sound, just a disconnect. I knew she was upset with me. I called back five more times. "We are too grown to act like that," Acting like what? I asked you a question, and you left me hanging," "I did not; don't you understand that I needed time to think?" "Now you had time, so what's the verdict?" "A good thing happened today," "What good thing?" "My parents would like to meet you," "Meet me for what?" "I told them about you so they would like to meet you," "I am not going to meet your parents when I am not your woman," "Who said you're not?" "You never asked me," "Okay, I am asking you now, will you be my woman?" "No," "No, why not?" "You're a man, and you should ask me to my face, not over the phone," "Okay, when will I see you face to face?" "You tell me I have to fly out to California next Friday," "Well, that gives you seven days if you want me; you'll get here fast," "Wow, okay, okay, I will come this weekend,"

After all the back and forth, we agreed to see each other on the weekend. I don't understand why I had to go through all of that. I believe Amelia was being difficult on purpose.

The following day, I received a phone call from the job I had interviewed for a week ago. The H.R. representative said, "I am sorry to inform you, but we have moved on with a better-qualified person for the job," I said, "Thank you for the phone call," I hung up abruptly. I didn't understand why they had to call me to tell me that shit. Needless to say, my heart was broken because of it. Being rejected for

## WHAT IT TAKES TO BE THE MAN

an opportunity is a challenge almost every black man goes through. It's hard to find and to keep a job in this world. I just shook my head and didn't let it get me down; at the end of the day, we all must keep pushing on. Maybe it was a blessing that they didn't hire me. That's how I had to look at it to cope with life's disappointments.

Hearing that news made me get into my writing even more. A simple no couldn't defeat me, and you won't get the job. I sat behind my computer and started writing until my mind was exhausted. I guess that's how I dealt with my stress and love for writing; I just created it until my mind couldn't stay awake.

I stayed in my house for a few days, doing nothing but eating and writing movie scripts. The weekend was now here, and it was time for me to see Amelia face to face. I didn't know the big deal about her not answering me over the phone, but women have a different way of doing things. I guess meeting face-to-face is more personal.

On my way to the house, it gave me time to think about where I was with myself in life. Maybe I didn't trust people enough because of what people have done to me in the past. Seeing my Momma cheating on my Dad always seemed to haunt me when it came to trying to build a relationship with a woman. Going through with what my cousin Harold put me through with sleeping with my ex-girlfriend Regina hardened my heart. And, with all the odds with Yvonne, I didn't want a relationship with Amelia to be a distraction.

# WHAT IT TAKES TO BE THE MAN

While going through all these thoughts, I realized I was my own worst enemy. As I thought about all these things, I saw police lights behind me. Immediately, my heart dropped, and fear came upon me. "What do they want?" "I hope they're not pulling me over," I said out loud. I started shaking from being nervous because any run-in with the police for a black man could be his last day on this earth. I took a deep breath, and I pulled to the side of the road.

Suddenly, the police car flew by me at a high speed with its lights and sirens on. I sat for a few minutes before I pulled off. I was so ecstatic when he didn't pull me over. It's sad to know you have to fear for your life every time the police pull you over, but this is the world we live in. The thought of the police driving behind me made me fearful, even though I hadn't done anything wrong. I was shaken up until I reached Ameila's house.

"Come in, DeVon, what's wrong with you, you look like you've seen a ghost?" "I am a little shaken up because I thought the police were about to pull me over,"

"You're legal and don't have a criminal record, so why were you worried?" "Where I am from, black men have always been worried about the police; you know I once sued a police precinct?" "No, I didn't know that,"

I told Amelia what happened in my past, and she sat in shock as I told her the stories and how innocent the police targeted black men.

## WHAT IT TAKES TO BE THE MAN

Amelia acted oblivious to my experience, and I guess that's because her family was well off and the fact that she was light-skinned from being bi-racial.

After I calmed down, Amelia went into the kitchen to get us a bottle of water, and then the more serious conversations began. I told her how I felt, and she shared her emotions. Even though I was ready to give in and commit, something in my gut kept aching my soul. As we conversed, I realized that my hesitation was because of my past, at least I had hoped.

I knew how much a commitment meant to Amelia, so my heart and mind said, what the hell, let's try this and see how it works out. I didn't want to give up on love, although I put those emotions and attachments on the back burner this far in my life. Finally, the time came; during a calm and quiet moment, I looked into Amelia's eyes and asked, "Amelia, will you be my woman?" Her eyes grew big, and she said without any more hesitation," "Yes, yes, yes, DeVon Edwin Bell, I will be your woman, but only if you will be my man, my king?" I responded, "Yes, I will, baby," We hugged and kissed.

We made love that night until the early morning hours. I was so exhausted about the time the sun came up. I got up to wash my face and brush my teeth, then laid back down. Amelia did the same. We slept for a few more hours. It was nearly 11 am when we got up to make breakfast together.

## WHAT IT TAKES TO BE THE MAN

After breakfast, we made plans for her to meet my parents that following Tuesday. "You're meeting my parents; when do you get to meet yours?" "That will have to be in the summer; they live out Midwest now," "They moved out west; when did that happen?" "It's a long story; I will tell you about it one day; for now, I will meet yours," Amelia said. It was odd that she hadn't told me much about her parents and their living out west. My next question was how she ended up in Upstate New York, but I didn't say anything to her. The date was made for her to meet Momma and Dad; they are hard on my female friends. I sure hope they like Amelia, I thought.

On my way home, my antennae started rising. I thought about Amelia and her saying that her parents weren't in New York. I wondered if she had ever mentioned that to me because if she did, I didn't recall. I believe that was something she should have told me. I wondered what else she was keeping from me. I stopped thinking about the situation when my phone rang.

"Hello, is this DeVon Edwin Bell?" "Yes, it is, who's speaking?" "I am Demetrius Dobson of Sanctuary Literary Agency, and I noticed you reached out to our office in an email a few months ago,"

"If I did, it probably was the end of last year, I am not sure," "You are Mr. Bell, though, correct?" "Yes, I am," "Okay, I just want to make sure, now, you have a movie script and is searching for an agent to represent you?" "Yes, I need an agent," "Are your scripts completed?" "Yes, they are." "May I ask you how many you have written?" "I have about twenty, now," "Wow, now that's impressive; when would you like to schedule a face-to-face appointment?" "Where are you located, Mr. Dobson?" "We are here in downtown Manhattan, New York," "I was down there a month or so ago," "Down here, where are you located?" "I am in Upstate, New York, but coming to the city isn't the problem." "That's good. So you are still seeking a presentation?" "I am not so sure; I have an appointment with an agency in California this weekend," "Way out west, well if that doesn't work out, this is my number, and I will email you my information, please, please get back to me, I would like to represent you," "Wow, this is crazy, but I will stay in touch," "Good, Mr. Bell, and one other thing," "What's that?" "Please send some transcripts of your work, and I will give you my honest opinion and what I feel needs to be corrected, free of charge," "Oh, wow, free of charge, all right, I will send you as soon as I get home," "Thank you, I look forward to speaking to you again one day," "Okay, I will send those transcripts later this evening, thank you," "No, thank you, Mr. Bell, I hope to talk to you soon, and good luck," "Thank you again, goodbye," I said as I hung up.

My heart started pounding hard, and butterflies filled my stomach. After all of this time, I felt like I was finally getting recognized. Agents rearching out to me was a big thing, especially when I think about everything I had to do to get to this place. I could've been in

## WHAT IT TAKES TO BE THE MAN

prison for selling drugs or something, but God gave me a better path, and now it was time to fulfill my destiny.

I called Momma and told her the good news. She and Dad were together and said they were proud of me. After I told them she would be over at Momma's house that Tuesday, they couldn't wait to meet Amelia. It seemed like everything was falling into place. Sometimes, having a little patience is all we need, and putting positive thinking out in the air is a way to motivate the universe to fulfill God's design; that's how I feel about life, my circumstances, shortcomings, and trying situations.

Tuesday finally came, and Amelia had the day off. We ate breakfast, walked in the park, and had a light lunch. I enjoyed every moment with her, and then it was time for us to head to my Momma's house. I was in good spirits. I prayed that everything would work out and that my parents would fall in love with Amelia.

Momma and Dad were waiting for us as we walked up the porch. They were smiling, and so was I. I introduced Amelia to them, and we all entered the house and sat down.

Conversations between Momma and Amelia seemed to go well. Dad and I conversed a little on the side. "She's a nice girl," Dad said. "Yes, she is, thank you, Dad," "You like her a lot?" "Something like that?" "What do you mean something like that?" "That's either a yes or no question," "Yes, Dad, yews, I do," "That's more like it. Are you sure this is the one?" "I am, I guess," "I am, I guess, what's going on, son?" "Nothing, Dad, I just don't fully trust anyone," "Then why are you getting into this relationship?" "Because I care about her, and she gave me an ultimatum." "If she had to do all that, then maybe you shouldn't rush into a commitment," "Dad, I already committed," "Just like you made it, you can change it, but do what's best for you; what do I know?" "You know a lot, Dad, and I trust your judgment. I want to give Amelia and me a chance; she deserves that, right, Dad?" "Everyone deserves a chance, but giving out charity in a relationship isn't good because people's emotions and feelings get involved, and she looks tough, fuck around, and that woman will kill you," "Dad, come on now, isn't that extreme," "No, but I am just saying be careful, and make sure she is the one," "I am Dad," I said.

Momma and Amelia kept talking, and Dad and I injected ourselves into their conversation. We laughed and watched movies, and everything seemed to click with my parents and Amelia.

After hours of chatting, Amelia was ready to go, and so was I. Momma and Dad asked her everything under the sun. As we were leaving, Momma said, "It was a pleasure to meet you, Amelia; maybe one day we can meet your parents,"

Ameila's expression changed, and she said, "Sure, I will let them know as soon as I see them; I mean, talk to them," I was shocked to hear her say that, knowing they were out in the Midwest. We got into my car, and I drove her back home. We didn't talk much, but she said she enjoyed my parents. I must admit she didn't sound all that excited. I wanted to question her about my Momma asking to meet her parents and her response, but I didn't want to mess up a beautiful day. I enjoyed her, and I thought the meeting with my parents was a good way for all of us to get closer.

As we approached Ameila's house, I told her about the other agent. She hugged me, praised me, and wished me the best.

# Chapter

# 21

## *Lining With The Stars*

I returned to Momma's house the following day to ask what she thought of Amelia. I was hurt knowing she didn't like or trust her.

"I don't trust that girl, DeVon," "Why do you say that, what did she do to make you feel that way?" "I would ask her questions, and then in the next sentence, she would say the opposite; I think she has trouble telling the truth,"

"Are you sure, Amelia very open woman, and she's an open book," "I believe she's open all right but not like you think; you know your Momma knows women because hell, I am a woman, and something not right about that girl, but hey, you chose her," "Come on Momma, give her some slack, you don't know her that well, maybe she will prove to you in time," I said. Momma gave me a dirty look and walked into the kitchen to make coffee. "Hello, hey, good morning," My Dad said as she walked into Momma's house. "Don't you ever knock," Momma chuckled.

"You are my wife still; we haven't gotten a divorce," Dad laughed. "And we are not either," Momma smirked. "Hello, Dad, so what did you think about Amelia yesterday?"

"I liked her, but it's you that I am worried about," Dad said. "Leave it up to your Dad; he likes anything in a shirt dress," Momma giggled. "What, stop that. She was a nice-looking girl, but I am not sure DeVon is ready for a woman like that," "A woman like what?" I said." "She seems to have herself together, and she is ready for you to commit to a higher level," Dad said.

"DeVon better not commit to that half-bred girl, and why didn't you tell her she has a white Momma and a black Daddy?" Momma asked. "Huh, because I didn't know that; I thought she was just a light-complexion woman," I said. "You mean you haven't met her parents?" Dad asked. "She's probably adopted or ran away from her parents," Momma said. "Now, why do you say that?" Dad asked. "Yes, why, Momma?" I asked. "The girl is a pathological liar; I can tell," Momma said. "Momma just doesn't like her Dad; she doesn't even know her," I said. "Boy, didn't I tell you Momma knows best, and that half-breed girl doesn't mean you any good," Momma said. "I wouldn't say all of

## WHAT IT TAKES TO BE THE MAN

that now; I thought Amelia was very respectful; she seemed to like DeVon," Dad said. "What do you know?" Momma said.

"Don't you two start; I think you need to give it time and get to know Amelia as I do, Momma, and then you might just change your mind," I said. "I am not thinking about your Momma," Dad said. "If you weren't thinking about me, why are you at my house?" Momma said.

Before Dad responded, I changed the subject and started discussing the movie on the TV. Momma and Dad went into the kitchen, and while they were talking about old times, I thought about how Momma felt about Amelia and that she was a liar. Again, my thoughts went back to the time Momma cheated on Dad while he was at work with that man. It started making sense for me to believe what she said about Amelia, but I wasn't entirely convinced she was right.

I am a man, and it's up to me to decide who I want to be with. It's not up to my mom or dad to tell me who to be with or fall in love with; that's my decision, and it's only mine. I took what they both said into consideration, and I took it with a grain of salt. A man must make his own decisions, and I stand by his good or bad choices, and that's what I intend to do.

I left Momma's house feeling certain, but I knew not to tell Amelia that Momma didn't like her, even though I think Dad liked her.

## WHAT IT TAKES TO BE THE MAN

I just prayed about it and hoped that Amelia would prove Momma wrong in time.

A few days passed, and I packed all my things and had Amelia drop me off at the airport. I kissed her, and she wished me the best. "Don't forget to tell that agent you have a friend looking for a representative," Amelia smiled.

"I will let him know," I yelled as I entered the airport terminal. I got my ticket, turned in my luggage, and sat. Since I was a couple of hours ahead of my flight, I sat and made calls, checked, and answered emails.

About an hour later, I got a phone call from Yvonne. "Where are you and are you coming to get your children this weekend?"

"No, I can't, I am on my way out of town,"

"Out of town, out of town for what?"

"I have an important appointment with an agent,"

"Are you still trying to be famous, that's what's wrong with all of you black men; you want the easy way out; you don't want to work like normal people do,"

"No, you can work for the Caucasians all you want; I want better for myself. I have a gift, so I'd rather bet on myself than go and work at some Caucasian's job,"

## WHAT IT TAKES TO BE THE MAN

"As I said, a lazy ass black man, you need to be here with your children," "I know where I need to be, and I don't appreciate you saying all this to me, when I tried to come and get them, you made all these excuses and now I am trying to do something positive, you are trying to destroy my dreams,"

"I am not trying to destroy your dreams, and all I am saying you, is you should be here with your children,"

"I love my children, and they know that; that's why I am doing this. I have some important people to meet, and I will be back in a week or so,"

"Never mind, and don't worry about your children; they will be just fine, I always make sure they are fine anyway,"

"And, so do I," "Man, whatever, I have to go to work now, make sure you call and check on them," "I was just about to," "You don't have to do it now, wait for about an hour and they will be over my sister's house," "Okay, I will call then, I am at the airport,"

"It's a shame you're going out of town and won't spend time with your children." "Bye, I have to go," I said, and Yvonne hung up. Sometimes, it's so hard to give her respect, but I know I have to because she's the Mother of my children. I never understood how she got this way or why she felt she had to hurt me. I could be like the Dads who never cared about their children, but instead, I am there for them and want to be around them. Maybe one day, God will humble her," I thought, as it was just about time for me to board my plane.

As I boarded the airplane, I found my seat in the back. There were lots of passengers on there. I put my luggage above my seat, sat down, and pulled out my computer.

I turned my phone on airplane mode as the plane took off. I started searching my computer as I embarked on my journey to California. Up until now, I had never been to the West Coast. I was excited and ready to take on any new adventure.

When the plane landed, I suddenly got cold feet. When I got my luggage, I called Uber. I had reservations at a nice hotel near the office, where I was set for my appointment.

I made it to the hotel a little late, and I was so tired from the three-hour behind time zone that I got in my room, showered, and fell asleep across the bed. I woke up the following morning and ran late for my appointment. I hurried, got some coffee, called for my rental car, and dressed well for the occasion.

I was lucky to make it to my appointment with minutes to spare. I was out of breath as I was able to walk into Mr. Matthew Granite's office. "Good morning, Mr. Bell. I see you made it to LA; how was your flight?" "Good morning, thank you, my flight was a long one, you know, with the three-hour time change, and that's why I was rushing and out of breath as I entered your office," "I bet you exhausted," "Yes, but I will okay, for now, that cup of coffee woke me up," "There's nothing like a good old cup of coffee," Mr. Granite said as his secretary called him on his phone. "Mr. Bell, Excuse me for a second," He said as I sat.

For about three minutes, all I heard Mr. Granite say on the phone was," Uh, yeah, that's right, that's right, ah, ah," I looked around his luxurious office and saw some bestselling author's pictures and magazine covers everywhere. I saw awards for Mr. Granite and some from the authors he worked with.

Suddenly he got off the phone and he said, "I am so sorry about that, sometimes, I have to do my secretary's job, but she's going through a change in life, she recently lost her husband in a car accident," "That's so sad," "Yes, it is, he was a good man to her, and now she's trying to heal," "She's probably still mourning," I said, "That's it, but enough talk about my secretary, I received some of your transcripts you emailed to me and I must say, I was very impressed, you have a way with words, and I can visualize seeing your script being featured in a big film," I said in shocked. "You can?" "Yes, I would like to shop your manuscript to some film producers in LA," "Wow, I can't believe this; thank you, this has always been a dream of mine," "Well, let's see if we can make your dream and reality and in the long run, make a lot of money together," "Now, that would be a blessing, you didn't know how much I have been trying to find someone to represent me," "If you trust me, I will make sure, you and your family will be in a great position to profit off your work," "So, what's next?" "Do you have a lawyer?" "Not as of this moment, but soon," "Okay, that's important; do all your work have copyrights?" "Yes, except the few that I am still working on now,"

"That's good; we will work on them when they are complete; next, I will create a package for your best manuscript and present it to some of the biggest film executives in the industry. I'll tell you what, give me a few days to get things together, and you find a lawyer, and we will work out a contract,"

"A few days?" "Yes, I need you here for at least a week; I can't promise anything is going to happen in a week, but let me check some leads. Plus, a few people owe me some favors,"

"Okay, I will extend my stay for this week; I am so excited; this just seems to be too good to be true and unreal," "It's real, and I will try my best to get your movie scripts sold at a good price,"

"Okay, that sounds good. I will be at my hotel working on some new projects, but right now, I am so hungry," "Yes, and get yourself something to eat; I will be in contact with you by tomorrow at least,"

"Okay, and I will look for a good lawyer; I am not sure if I should get one here in LA or New York," If I were you, I would get one where you live; we can always have Zoom meetings and fax contracts over online,"

"That's right, okay, let me get out of here; I have to let my lady know about this," "Yes, Mr. Bell, go share the news," Mr. Granite said as he showed me to the door. I felt good about everything, so I left his office in a perfect mood. I called Momma and Dad and told them I had to stay in LA for a week longer. Momma didn't like that idea for some reason, but wasn't she the one who said I might have to leave New York and venture out? I was a little confused, but as my Dad talked to me, he gave me the support to uplift my spirits, and that's what I needed.

I called Amelia as I made it to downtown LA. I was hungry, so I needed to get something to eat. I stopped at Joyce Soul and Sea as Amelia discussed my appointment with Mr. Granite.

"You think it went well," Amelia asked with excitement. "Yes, he's going to create a package for me to give to the film producers," "What kind of package?" "I guess with all my content like my transcripts, manuscripts, query letter, I am now sure, but he's going to get back to me soon," "Wow, I am so happy for you," "Thank you, but it's a little early for celebrations," "No, it's not, you have this tied up, I believe in you," "Thanks, Mr. Granite did say, I need a lawyer, so, I have to start trying to find one," "That's good you will find one, and don't forget to tell him about me," "I won't but let me get my foot in

# WHAT IT TAKES TO BE THE MAN

the door first," Amelia paused for a second and then she said, "Okay, all right, I got you,"

The tone of her voice didn't sound very excited at that point. After that, she didn't say much, so I told her I had to go because my food was getting cold. I didn't mean to offend Amelia, but she took what I said wrong.

I finished eating my food and went to the jewelry store in downtown LA. There was a lot of hype about their jewelry district. As I was walking, I was still deep in thought about how Amelia shut down on me. I am only trying to get my foot in the door first; am I wrong for that?

## Chapter

# 22

## *Escaped Unscathed*

While walking and wondering if I had said anything wrong to Amelia, I approached Helms Street Jeweler, one of the famous jewelry stores in downtown LA. Because of my thoughts, I was unaware of what was happening in front of me.

As I approached the front entrance, I heard a commotion. I heard glass breaking and men's jewelry, "Get on the fucking ground, get down," "I want you to give me everything in your fucking cash register," A man's voice yelled.

Six men dressed in all black with large guns were robbing the jewelry store. They were wrecking the place and causing havoc. I stood motionless as I was caught right in the middle. I tried to slowly back out of the store as one of the men grabbed all the jewelry from the display case.

"Hold up, you, get your ass down, do you want to get your fucking brains blown out?" One of the gunmen screamed. "I don't see a thing, I don't see a thing," I yelled as I kneeled.

"Let's go, let's go," One of the robbers yelled.

"I should kill your fucking ass," The gunmen screamed.

"Please don't; I promise I didn't see a thing; I have children, I have children," I said aloud.

The gunmen cocked his gun on me and aimed his gun at my head. My heart started pumping out of control at that moment, and I started pleading with him. All I could think about was my children and family.

"I understand why you are doing this, and I used to be just like you; please don't kill me; my children need me," I pleaded.

"Let's go, let's go, now," The head robber said. The gunmen pulled his gun off my head, and he said, "Today is your lucky day," He ran out of the jewelry store with the rest of his gang.

The owner of the jewelry store hit the alarm, and he called the police. The robbers fled in a black van. You could hear the tires screech, and they did a wild U-turn and sped off.

## WHAT IT TAKES TO BE THE MAN

"Sir, are you all right?" The Jewelry asked.

"I, I, I think so; I am a little shaken up, and I, I, think I'm okay," I said as I felt my pants. I was so damn scared that I pissed in my pants. I couldn't believe that I was in the middle of a robbery, and I almost got my head blown off; I nearly lost my life.

I started leaving the store in disbelief at what had just happened. "Sir, can you stay and be a witness?" the jeweler asked.

"I am not from here; I am sorry, I can't; I have to go," I said as I ran out of the store. "But, sir, sir," The jeweler yelled as he followed me.

"I can't. I can't stay," I yelled as I fled. I hurried and made it back to the hotel. It took a while for my brain to catch up to my body. I was terrified. For some reason, that gunmen spared my life; he could've ended all of my dreams and taken a good father from his children, but he didn't. I felt grateful to God because he must have heard my prayers while I was begging for my life.

As I sat in my hotel room shaking and praying, I turned on the TV. I was surprised that the robbers had gotten away with 1.2 million in cash and jewelry, and the robbery was caught on camera. I could see my head down as the video was rolling. The reports asked if anyone knew who I was because they couldn't clearly describe me. Then I heard another reporter say, "That bystander must have been scared for his life, but for some reason, the robbers spared his life; he must be a lucky man; the police say the robbers are still at large, but they do have some leads." Those robbers were young, and I could tell they were young black men. I knew I couldn't snitch to the police; that was always a code of the streets. Even though I am no longer in the streets, snitching is one of the codes to live by, and the police never gave me a reason to help them with anything; they only brought terror and disruption into our neighborhoods.

I will never forget what the police did to me in the past, so there was no way I was helping them with their investigation. I had to sue them for the trauma they caused me. I never had to steal anything, but those robbers came there for business; their sole mission was to take everything. I've been in their shoes, as you have to do anything to survive. I am not saying what they did was right, but sometimes, in life, your circumstances cause you to do some crazy ass shit. I was just happy that my life was spared.

I didn't want to tell Momma or Dad because they would like me to get on that plane immediately. I called Amelia and told her what had happened. "Are you okay, are you all right, they did catch them, right?" "Amelia, to tell the truth, I am not so sure, but one thing I do know is that I was lucky," "You must have been terrified," "After all I have done in the streets, this was the first time, I feared that I wouldn't make it, he had a gun pointed at my head," "And, what did you do?" "I pleaded with him," "And that's why he let you live, it wasn't your time to die and leave your family,"

"I guess not, the police were looking for me to ask me questions," "Ask you questions for what, you weren't involved," "No, they wanted witnesses; the video shows I wasn't involved, well, it showed a man with his head down," "They didn't see your face?" "No, that's why they were asking if anyone sees me, to tell me to contact them," "Are you going to contact them?" "No, I am not a snitch," "But, DeVon, they could've taken your life," "But they didn't," "If I were you, I would help the police," "I will never help the police, they weren't good to me or my family in the past,"

"I think you should, but it's your choice if you don't want to,"

"I don't because the next thing you know, they'll be acting like I was a part of the robbery as if I was a part of the plan; I don't trust the police," "Okay, I understand, but," Amelia said as I cut her off. "I have to get some sleep. I will talk to Mr. Granite tomorrow, and hopefully, I can be on a plane and on my way home by the weekend."

"Okay, good night, be careful; I am praying for you," "Thank you, I need all of the prayers I can get; good night," She said as we hung up. I laid back on the bed, and I stared at the ceiling as tears started flowing out of my eyes; damn, I was lucky.

## WHAT IT TAKES TO BE THE MAN

I thought, what would have happened if they had killed me? My family and children would be devasted. The one reason I got out of the streets was because of the love of my loved ones. It could've all been taken from me in an instant. I am grateful that God is still walking with me, even though I am starting a perfect man. I couldn't sleep well that night, so I watched the news until early morning, and finally, I fell asleep just as the sun rose. I woke up at about 11 am because my phone rang. "Hello," I said groggily.

"I am sorry did I wake you?"

"Who is this, no, no, it's okay, but who am I speaking to?"

"This is Matthew Granite, how are you?"

"I am exhausted, and I went through an ordeal yesterday,"

"I am sorry to hear that, but I was calling you to let you know that I ran into some roadblocks and it will take me longer to shop your project,"

"How much longer?" "I am not sure. Do you think you can stay for another week or so?" "Another week or so, no, I don't think so," "Okay, I understand, but you are staying the rest of this week, correct?" "I am leaving Friday morning; my plane leaves at 10:30 am," "All right, I should hear something by then, but if not, I will be in your city next month, and we can always do work through email and Zoom meetings," "Are you sure you can represent me?" "Of course, I just have some other projects I'm working on as well," Mr. Granite said.

At this point, I felt Mr. Granite was giving me the runaround, or maybe he was too busy. "Do you know of anyone else who wants a representation?" He asked. I paused for a moment, and then I thought about Amelia. "Yes, I do, as a matter of fact, but I was hoping you would be my representation first," "You are most definitely first; I am working on your project; don't give up on me yet," "I am not giving up on you, but it seems as if you already have a lot on your plate," "Believe me, it's not that, I am just waiting to talk to the right people," "Okay, I will send you her information and did you say you will be in my city next month?"

"Yes, they are having a film fair there, didn't you know?"

"No, I didn't because my city doesn't host things like that, often," "Well, now they are, and I will be there; hopefully, we will meet for some good news," "Well, email me the information, and I will be there also," I said. "Okay, now you said she is thus a female screenwriter?" "Yes, it is, her name is Amelia," "Amelia, okay, let her know that I am interested in meeting her and seeing her work," "Okay, I will make sure she gets the message, but if you can't represent me, please let me know," Mr. Bell, please don't worry, I will make sure you get the best deal for your project," "Thank you," I said as we hung up.

## WHAT IT TAKES TO BE THE MAN

The next couple of days, I barely left my hotel room, only to go out and eat at a nearby restaurant. I do not want to take any more chances in these streets of LA. It was bad enough that all this chaos happened in the heart of downtown.

I stayed laser-focused on creating new projects. I didn't hear from Mr. Granite, so I guess he was out trying to shop for my project. The last night I was in LA, I went into the lobby, sat at the bar, and had beer. I was people-watching and also cautious of what was happening around me.

Suddenly, a young Caucasian couple came and sat next to me. The couple sounded distraught. "We were so damn lucky to get out of there," The young lady said. "Yes, we were; I can't believe they shot that man," The young man said.

The both of them kept talking about something happening in a hotel, so I politely asked them, "Excuse me, I don't mean to listen to your conversation, but did you say someone got shot in the hotel?"

"Yes, oh hi, no problem, I am Gage, and this is Serene; it wasn't this hotel, thank God, but we just left a hotel where a gunman was shooting down people from the tenth floor," Serene said.

"The place was chaotic, and everyone was screaming and yelling," Gage said. "And running," Serene said.

"Say what, that's crazy; I see a lot goes on in LA," I said.

# WHAT IT TAKES TO BE THE MAN

"Oh, you're not from LA?" Gage asked. "No, I am from Upstate New York?" I said. "What brings you out here?" Serene asked.

"I am a screenwriter trying to sell my movie scripts," I answered. That's cool. Have you had any luck so far?" Gage asked. "At this point, I am not sure, but tell me more about the shooter," I interrupted.

"Oh yeah, back to the story; I saw the squat team go up the stairs with guns with red beams on them," Seren said.

"I heard them screaming at the guy," Gage said. "What were they saying?" I asked. "I heard them tell him to put his hands up; I could hear him say they are up; please don't kill me," Gage said.

"I have never been so terrified; I kept telling Gage we need to get our things and find another hotel," Serene said.

"I know, but they weren't letting anyone upstairs; the Squat team blocked all the exits, and then they told everyone downstairs to go outside," Gage said. "That must have been terrifying," I said. "What's your name, Sir?" Gage asked. "Oh, I am sorry for not introducing myself; I am DeVon Edwin Bell," I said as I sipped my drink.

"It's a pleasure to meet you, but as soon as we got a chance, we got our things and came to this hotel," Serene said.

"I heard that the guy didn't comply with the police, and they shot and killed him; I am glad we got out of there," Gage said.

## WHAT IT TAKES TO BE THE MAN

"That is crazy; it's a good thing no one else lost their life," I said. "That's true, are you here in LA by yourself?" Serene asked. "Yes, but I am leaving in the morning," I said. "I don't blame you; we are staying until Sunday; we live in Utah, but we visit here all the time; Serene's parents live here," Gage said.

"It's getting late; let me finish this drink; it was nice to meet the two of you; this hotel should be safe," I said. "Thank you, and good luck to you; I hear a lot of writers, actors, and actresses come here to make it in Hollywood," Gage said. "Yes, I hear a long list," I said. "You seem like a nice guy; maybe you'll be the next big filmmaker," Serene said.

"That's a big maybe, but thanks for telling your story at the hotel," I said. "Hey, you might be able to write a story about it," Serene said. "Maybe I will go to my room and watch it on the news," I said. "It should be on there," Gage said. "Well, Mr. Bell, it was nice to meet you; we both need a drink," Serene said. I finished my drink and said my goodbyes to Gage and Serene. They were an interested couple. I returned to my room, packed my things, and prepared for bed.

As I lay in bed, I thought about the ordeal they went through with the gunmen at that hotel, and it made me think of all the craziness in the world. Maybe I should write about it, I thought. I turned on the TV and watched the news until the scary scene of the gunmen being shot

## WHAT IT TAKES TO BE THE MAN

by police was there for the world to see. It was like a scene out of a movie. When I saw that, I knew I had to write that story. The police shot that man in cold blood, and he had no weapons on him.

# Chapter

# 23

## *Deceit Unveiled*

I got all my things the following day and headed to the airport. I was so happy to get the hell out of LA. I texted my Momma and my Dad to let them know I was on my way home. I called Amelia, but she didn't answer her phone.

Mr. Granite called before I took off from the flight. "Hello, Mr. Bell; sorry I couldn't get you connected with anyone yet, but please be patient, are you still here in LA?" "I have been patient, but I am at the airport and about to board my flight," "That's okay; I will be in touch by phone and by email; as I said, I will be in your city in a couple of weeks or so, and we will touch basis then and don't forget to send me your friend's info, the other writer, that you told me about," "My plane is here, we will talk soon," I said as I hung up the phone.

Mr. Granite seems shady to me. As he had promised, I didn't get any feedback from anyone. I started to think he was a fraud or playing with my mind.

Something in my gut told me to keep looking for literary agents. I was always taught to listen to that little voice in my head. Mr. Granite seemed shiesty, and I may find out in due time. As I reached the end of my flight, I called Amelia, and she finally picked up the phone.

"Hello, hey, I called you earlier, but I didn't get any answer,"

"Devon, I was kind of busy, but I didn't hear the phone anyway, are you on your way back?"

"Oh, okay, yes, I should be there in an hour, can you please pick me up from the airport?"

"Sure, I will be there; how was the trip? Are there any leads?" "My trip was a learning experience, but I don't have any real leads yet; I am waiting for Mr. Granite to call me,"

"Okay, is that the literary agent you were scheduled to see?"

"Yes, Mr. Granite said he will be in our city in a couple of weeks, and hopefully, he'll have some good news; he also asked if I knew anyone else who was a writer, and I said yes,"

## WHAT IT TAKES TO BE THE MAN

"You told him about me?" "Not so much so, yet, but he wants me to send him your email and information so he can talk to you,"

"He does, did you give it to him?" "Not yet, but I will if he calls me back," "What do you mean if?" "Nothing, I am just waiting patiently," "That's exciting, aren't you excited?" "I will be excited when someone gets me a deal with my movie script,"

"DeVon, stop being so negative, it's not appealing at all,"

"I am not being negative; I am being real; I will not get too excited, only to be let down," "Whatever, I am excited for you, then, okay, I will be at the airport in an hour," "Okay, I will see you then," "DeVon, please give that literary agent my information, this could be both of our big breaks," Amelia said.

When I hung up with her, Mr. Granite called and said he had some leads and would get back to me in a few days. That made me feel a little better because up until then, I felt my trip was for nothing, and I almost got myself killed at that jewelry store in LA.

Mr. Granite asked about another writer before I got off the phone, so as soon as I hung up with him, unreluctantly, I sent him Ameila's email address and phone number.

As the plane landed, my phone rang, and it was Yvonne. I dreaded answering the phone because all she did was complain, but I did it because it could be an emergency for my children. "Hello," I said.

## WHAT IT TAKES TO BE THE MAN

"DeVon, where are you, are you back from your trip?" "I actually just landed," "Damn, okay, then you can't watch your children tonight, can you?" "Not tonight, I am too exhausted," "You can never do anything for your children," "Hey, that's not true, my plane just landed, I was in LA, and it's a three-hour difference," "I don't give a damn about that," "Anyways, so what are you going to do?"

"I can't do anything but take them to my sister's house," "Your sister lives in a bad neighborhood; it's ghetto over there," "So what, you are from the ghetto, and so now, you are all high and mighty,"

"Whatever, no I am not, it's just dangerous as hell over your sister's house," "Don't worry about it, you are not here to watch them,"

"I can watch them tomorrow." "Don't bother; I will handle it." "I don't need you to handle anything," I said as I heard the ringtone.

I grunted and yelled as I got off the plane. That woman knows how to push my damn buttons. I thought by the time I received my luggage, Amelia was already outside waiting for me.

"Hey there, how, how long have you been out here?"

"I just pulled up; well, I had to drive around a few times because this police won't let you park here; boy, they are strict," "Yes, I know; why are you all smiles?" I asked. "That guy called me and emailed me," "What guy?" "That agent, uhm, Mr. Matthew Granite, the same man you went to see in LA," "He did, already, damn that was fast, and

# WHAT IT TAKES TO BE THE MAN

what did he say?" "He was asking questions about my work and said he would be here to talk to me in person when he comes into the city in a few weeks." And that's all?" "Yes, that was pretty much it," "I thought he would've asked you a lot more," I said, but Amelia sat quietly.

On the way home, I told Amelia everything that happened in LA, and she was surprised and horrified at the same time,"

"You could have been killed, and I don't know if I wanted to go to LA," Amelia frowned.

"It was scary, but I made it, and I was happy as hell to leave,"

"I bet you're not going back there,"

"I hope not," I chuckled.

"I need to stop by my house before I take you home. Is that okay?"

"Sure, why, what's wrong?"

"Nothing; I just need to get something, that's all."

"Okay," I said as we headed to Ameila's house. "I have to use the bathroom so bad," Amelia said as we approached her house. "Go ahead," "DeVon, you can come in because I don't know how long I will take," "Okay, are you sure you are okay?" "Yes, why do you ask me that? On that note, never mind, let me get here," She said as she unlocked the door. I followed close behind, walked into the living, and sat down. "Hurry up, girl," I chuckled. "Shut up," Amelia said as she zipped the zipper down her jeans and ran into the bathroom. I laughed while watching her move a hundred miles an hour to the toilet.

Since Amelia took a while to exit the bathroom, I got up and walked into her computer room. I remembered I had lost my flash drive, so I started looking behind the desk and on the floor. I searched behind the garbage cans and all the cords under the desk, but there was still nothing. I noticed a flash drive on Ameila's old computer when I left the room. Her old computer was hidden under notepads and a tablet.

I was just about to look at the flash drive, and Amelia came out of nowhere. She startled me. "What are you doing here? Are you ready to go?" "Oh, I was just looking at your computers because I need a new one myself," "Oh, yes, they are quite expensive now. Are you ready?" "Yes, I know they are, but yes, let's get out of here, nice computer," I said. "Thanks," Amelia said as he grabbed my arm and pulled me out of the room. That looked like my flash drive, but I still wasn't sure. "Why would Amelia steal my flash drive? No, that probably wasn't it," I said as we drove to my house.

"Were you searching for something?" Amelia said out of the clear blue sky. "Searching, what are you talking about? Was I searching for what?" "You were in my computer room, and you didn't ask me if I could go in there," "I didn't know I had to get permission," "Well, it is my house," "You are right, but no, as I said I was just looking at your computers," "That sounds crazy because you've seen them several times," "I was just curious," "Curious about what?" Amelia kept asking me the same questions repeatedly.

I was so happy to make it home. "Let me get back home; I have some things to do," Amelia said as she dropped me off in front of my apartment.

"Are you sure you don't want to come in?" "No, no, today, I have some things to do," "Okay, you know I do miss you; I thought maybe you could, you know, make love to me; I am horny," "Not now, I am on my monthly, I am sorry, I have to go DeVon," "All right, all right," I said as I took my luggage out of her back seat. "Bye, I will talk to you later," I said, and Amelia sped off.

For some reason, Amelia was acting strange. She was cold and less receptive to me than before. What's wrong with that woman? I thought.

I went into my apartment, put my things away, and thought about my trip and how Amelia acted towards me. I decided to head over to my Momma's house to see what she was up to. I knew Momma would be full of questions about my trip and Dad.

When I got to Momma's house, she walks out the door with a distraught look. "What's wrong, Momma?"

"Oh, hey DeVon, I see you made it back, it's your Aunt Ella,"

"What about her? She's not starting any fights with you anymore, has she?"

"No, she's locked up in jail again,"

"For what this time?"

"The same thing as last time, she got caught selling her ass, again by the police, this time he was an undercover police officer,"

"Why does she keep doing that crazy shit?"

"It's those drugs or the medicine that she's on; when Ella takes them meds, she's okay, but when Ella takes the meds and the drug together, she hit them streets doing crazy shit,"

"Well, I hope she can be saved. " "Nothing can save that crazy girl. I have to pick up your Grandmother; she's going with me."
"Okay, where are Ella's children?"

"Their other Grandmother has them; you know Carlton's side of the family,"

"Yes, I know, okay, well, I guess I am going back home,"

"You can stay here if you want; I won't be gone long. I want to hear about your trip; your Dad should be here in an hour," "Okay, I will wait here; I might nap. I am exhausted," I said as Momma left hastily. Not much longer after Momma left, Dad pulled up. "Hey, DeVon, I see you are back from your trip, and I'm glad you are safe and back in one piece."

"Dad, I am fortunate to make it back with my life; those people are crazy," "But you did get something accomplished, right?"

"Truthfully, I am not sure, Dad; I met with this literary agent named Matthew Granite, and he gave me the run-around, it seems,"

"I know it feels like that, son, but sometimes, you just have to have faith and not stop what you are doing; either way, I am proud of you, son; you could've ended up like some of your friends, in jail or dead, you know what I am saying, right?"

"I understand wholeheartedly; I am trying to do something with my life; every time I look around, everyone is doubting us black men; we are only looked at by society as criminals, and I admit at one time in my life, I lived in that hood mentality box, but as I grew older, I knew I had to do better."

"That's right, son, the Bible says when a man matures, he puts away childish things, and I believe you are growing into that man; never let anyone or anything stop you from what God has for you; now you know I am not a saint, but I do believe there is a God and I have prayed that he keeps you on a straight and narrow and narrow path, you will be okay,"

## WHAT IT TAKES TO BE THE MAN

"Thank you, Dad, I appreciate that," I said. Dad and I conversed more about my trip and a little bit about Amela. He was very interested in how she felt about me and my dreams.

I didn't get to tell him much because the doorbell rang, and it was my cousin Vanessa. She walked into the house, wiping tears. Vanessa still hadn't heard from Harold, and I could tell it was taking a toll on her. Her hair was wild, her face ashy, and Vanessa looked like she hadn't slept in weeks.

"Hi, Vanessa," Dad said as he hugged her. Hello, you two. Still nothing, but I have been hearing some rumblings in the streets," she said as she wiped her tears. I haven't heard anything either, plus I just got back into town," I said.

Suddenly, Vanessa started shaking and crying uncontrollably, "My son, my son, I won't even be able to bury him; who did this to him?" She screamed. I went over to hug her and said, "I don't know, I really don't know; are the authorities still looking for Harold?" I asked. "No, they have stopped, and so have the police; I just don't know what to do; he was my only son, she cried. "Now, this is sad; we are all hurting; we are sorry you are going through this," Dad said with a sad look.

"Have you heard anything? I asked. "No, but someone said Harold may be buried behind a house in one of those buried neighborhoods," "What?" Dad said. "I am sorry, I heard that too," "I wouldn't know where to look if that's true," She said. "Neither would I," I said. Vanessa stayed for a little while. Momma was taking too long to return home, so eventually, after chatting with Dad and me about Harold, she decided to go out and search for clues before going home.

"Bye, Vanessa, I said as she got into her car. "Bye, wish me luck," She said as she started to pull off. "Bye, Vanessa," Dad yelled as she pulled off.

"That is a sad situation, not knowing if your son is alive or dead; I feel so sorry for her," Dad said. "I do too; I mean, Harold is my cousin; we went through some bad times, and we weren't speaking for a while, but he did come back and apologized to me for the past,"

"I think I remember that day you were here, right?" Dad asked. "Yes, I wouldn't wish this on my worst enemy; I hope Vanessa holds it together," I said.

"Me too; I know it's hard for a parent to lose their child like this, and she doesn't even know where he is. I couldn't imagine losing you in that manner; I would go crazy," Dad said.

"This has to be so hard on her," I said. "All our lives, all we want is for our children to do well in life; it's already hard because we are black, but to be taken out of this world like that is horrible," Dad said with empathy. "You think he's dead, don't you, Dad?" "Yes, I do; he

## WHAT IT TAKES TO BE THE MAN

loved Vanessa; there ain't no way he would be gone this long; I don't care what kind of argument they had," "That's true, Dad, I pray she finds the answers she is looking for," I said. "Well, DeVon, I have to get out of here; your Momma is taking too long; tell her I will be back tomorrow," "Okay, Dad, I will talk to you tomorrow," "Okay, keep your head up and pray, God, is with you on your journey," Thank you Dad," "That's what I am here for, and that's to uplift my son, not everyone has a father that cares," He said. "Especially us black families, I am grateful to have you in my life, Dad; you have taught me a lot," "That's what all black Dads should do, but we will talk tomorrow; love you, son," "I love you too, Dad, bye," I said as he went and got into his car.

As Dad drove away, I felt grateful to have him in my life. I know so many of my friends and male cousins didn't have their Dads in their lives, and they have gone down the wrong path. Having a strong black king like my Dad is my blessing, and I will always honor him.

# Chapter

# 24

## *A Dual Reflection*

After Dad left, I fell asleep right there on the sofa. I was awakened by Momma when she came into the house. She had a lot to talk about because she seemed furious. I sat on the sofa, wiped my eyes with my hand, and yawned.

"Momma, why did it take you so long? Where is Ella?"

"Boy, you have to hear this story; your Aunt has lost her damn mind for real this time," "What happened?" "Your Grandmother and I went to pick her up from the police precinct, and as we were trying to get her to see what she was doing wrong by telling her to stop doing the drugs and selling her body, she started talking to herself," "Say what?" "Yes, she started saying crazy shit, so your Grandmother and I told her, if she kept talking to herself, we were going to take her ass to the crazy hospital for mental patients,"

"Momma, what she saying?" "Ella started saying the female deputies at the precinct were jealous of her and that they stole her hair and her pussy," "Huh, say what stole her what?" "You heard me, she said the female deputies stole her hair and her pussy,"

I chuckled and then said," What is wrong with her? She has really lost her mind," "Those drugs are affecting her, and she hasn't been taking her medicine," "Where is she now?" "That's what I was going to tell you; that damn girl jumped out of a moving car on Main Street, and we couldn't catch her," "Say what?" "You heard me; she jumped out of the car and almost got hit by the cars going in the opposite direction," "I guess she didn't want to go back to that mental hospital," "I guess not, they must have done something to her there, but she needs help, that bitch is crazy," Momma said.

"Momma, you are wrong for that," I said. "DeVon, I want to say something to you, not to change the subject or anything, but I want you to know that I am sorry for what Ella did to you as a child; I wish you had told me," I paused for a second, took a deep breath and said, "I know I should have told you, but I was scared you would've killed her," "And, if you had told me, I would have fucked her up,"

"That's why I didn't tell you; I was terrified, and I really didn't know what was going on," "You were too young to know; I am sorry, son; maybe that's why God is giving her back karma because what she did to you as a child," "I am not going to lie, I have thought about that too, she had it going on good for a while but now Ella's on drugs, lost her mind and selling her body, and has lost it all," "God doesn't play, and now she is feeling his wrath, I am so, so sorry, you had to go through that, I can't do anything about it now, but if you had told me then, I would have worn her ass out and probably killed her," "I know Momma, it had affected me mentally and sexually sometimes, but I don't want to talk about it, it was a long time ago," I said, and Momma got very quiet.

I immediately changed the subject and told Momma about Vanessa stopping by. We talked for over an hour about Harold's disappearance and what it was doing to Vanessa.

"It's a sad situation; I will call her tonight to check on her, so tell me about your trip," Momma said. I told her about the trip, and she was displeased I didn't get anything out of it. I didn't tell her about almost getting my head blown off during a robbery because that would only worry her, so I stayed away from that subject.

"What's up with you and that Amelia girl?" "Nothing, we are still an item," "I thought you would have liked her by now, I said in a low tone. "I told you she's no good for you," "I know you did, but I need to find out myself," "A hard head makes a soft ass," "Momma, you just don't like the girl," "What did I tell you, I am a woman to and a woman knows another woman and her intentions aren't good," "You would probably say that about any woman because I am your son," "No, not really, well, if I know that their energy isn't good, of course, I am going to say something," "Momma, she's okay, you don't have anything to worry about, you'll see," "If you say so," Momma said. I changed the subject once again while she was talking.

"Dad came by also," "He did; when did he leave?" "He left about forty-five minutes before you got here; he said he will be back tomorrow," "Okay, I am tired; I am about to take a nap, will you be here when I get up," Momma asked. "No, I am about to go home, and as a matter of fact, I am going to call Amelia on my way home," "That girl isn't any good," Momma said as she headed upstairs to her bedroom. I shook my head from side to side, and I left.

At this point, I felt no one would ever be good for me in my Momma's eyes. She is too overprotective, as far as I am concerned. On my way home, I couldn't help but think about everything Momma was saying about Amelia, so I decided to give her a call. I must have called and let the phone ring several times, but Amelia never answered.

I finally left a message and asked her to call me back when she could. While awaiting her call, I drove around the city and remembered what I had done in the past. The past has a funny way of reminding you where you come from.

## WHAT IT TAKES TO BE THE MAN

I drove down the neighborhoods that helped groom me as a young boy, and the crazy thing is, I noticed a few guys around my age still hanging out with young boys from a different generation. I think sometimes in life, the environment doesn't let some individuals grow, or they are afraid to grow up themselves; I didn't want to judge them because getting away from what you are used to can sometimes be scary. I just waved at them, and I kept it moving.

As I headed home, I thought about my children. I wanted the best for them, so I tried hard to be a role model. I had wished I could spend more time with them, but Yvonne wouldn't let that happen. How could she be so cold towards me and not allow me to see them? I never understood her motives, and it crushed me inside to know that my children were in the same city and I couldn't get them when I wanted to see them.

Maybe, just maybe, I chose the wrong woman to have my children with. That's something I can't change. Sometimes, your past follows you and haunts you even when trying to better yourself. I was in my thoughts and feelings but snapped back into reality as I made it home. Life is a struggle, and I must do my best to maintain through the good and the bad. The bad always seem to have a strong hold on you, but prayer is it's kryptonite.

## WHAT IT TAKES TO BE THE MAN

When I got into my house, I called Amelia several times, but her phone went to voicemail. What is wrong with that woman? I asked myself.

I didn't let it bother me. I turned on my computer, read some emails, and sent a few more to literary agents. I noticed an email from Matthew Granite and it read: "Mr. Bell, I am still trying to sell your manuscript, and it seems that your story isn't reaching the right film producers; I guess they are looking for something else, but don't you give up, I have some hookups that I am checking in when I come to New York, I will keep in touch, and oh, thank you for linking me up to Amelia, I will talk to you soon,"

I sat at my computer and thought," What does he mean link up with Amelia? He must have meant linking up with another writer like me." I let those negative thoughts go right out of my head. I got up after that and took my shower, and then I lay across my bed with my phone in my hand. I called Amelia again, and finally, she answered.

"Hello stranger, how are you doing? I have been calling you," "I have been sick with the flu; I am sorry I couldn't answer; I just started feeling better," "How long have you been sick?" "A little over a week,"

"I hope you feel better." "I am a lot better, so what is going on with you?" "Amelia, I have been trying to keep a positive mind about getting into the film industry, but it's not going anywhere,"

## WHAT IT TAKES TO BE THE MAN

"Don't think like that. I talked to Matthew, and he said he is still shopping your project; I sent him one of mine, and Matthew loved it, so it looks like he will be shopping both of our works,"

"He said that?" "Yes, he liked my work as well." "He actually said he's shopping for my project; did that come out of his mouth?" "Not in so many words, but I do believe he is; he's a very nice guy,"

"I am glad you think so because I thought he was giving me the runaround," "From what I got from him is that it's a competitive industry, and sometimes things take time,"

"I do understand that, but damn, give a brother a break,"

"DeVon, have patience; your time is coming, and so is mine,"

"I don't have anything but patience. I am happy, and I am proud of you. Hopefully, he can help both of us,"

"I believe he will, so what's happening with your family? Have you seen your children?" "No, not yet." "Why not? Are you still having problems with who you know?" "Yvonne is sometimes crazy; I don't know her problem." "She probably wants you back and misses a good thing." "Hell no, why would you say that?" "I know how us women are," Amelia said.

That reply reminded me of what Momma said about Amelia: that a woman knows another woman. I don't understand why Amelia said that, but it made me think about how she acted the last few weeks. Could Momma be right about Amelia?

I changed the subject because Amelia kept insinuating that Yvonne still loves me and wants me back. It almost seemed she was trying to push me back into Yvonne's arms.

"So, how are your parents?" I asked, and Amelia got quiet.

"Hello," I said. Oh, my parents are just fine. I talked to my Mother yesterday. "You did. I thought you were sick with the flu?" "I was, I mean, I am. We just spoke briefly. "Okay, are they coming to see you?" "My parents are too busy. " What parent is too busy to see their child when sick?"

"It's a long story," Amelia started coughing.

"Are you sure you're okay?"

"Yes, I have to take some more medicine, and I am going to lie back down. I will talk to you tomorrow," Amelia said as we hung up.

WHAT IT TAKES TO BE THE MAN

# Chapter

# 25

*Disloyal and Betrayed*

When Amelia and I hung up the phone, I thought she was a very secretive woman. Why does she keep everything with her parents a damn secret? **It made me wonder about her!**

I stayed up most of the night trying to figure out Amelia. I even started writing a character for her in my manuscript. I usually don't write about people in my personal life, but she started acting strange.

The following morning, I woke up, and I first tried to call Amelia. Once again, she didn't answer the phone. It bothered me how far apart it seemed as if she and I were going.

## WHAT IT TAKES TO BE THE MAN

I tried not to worry too much about it. I didn't want to get writer's block, but worrying about her was a distraction. I did what I always do, and that was to get on my computer and start writing. I was deep in a zone for at least an hour, and my phone rang. "DeVon, when are you coming by to see your children?" "Yvonne, I've been trying to see my children, but you are always making excuses," "What excuses, man, stop lying," "Lying, who's lying?" "You are; now, when are you coming?" "I will come to get them around 4 pm," "I didn't say come get them; I said come see them because I have to go to work, and after that, I am taking them to my sister's house so she can watch them while I'm at work,"

"How many times have I told you I don't like them to go over there? It's too damn ghetto, and they are shooting and shit," "I don't care what you told me; that's where they will be, shit, you don't want to watch them," "Who said that, and where did you get that from?" "I said it: every time I ask you, you are always doing something," "Well, sometimes, I am busy; you can always take them to Momma's house; she would love to see them and spend time with them," "Never mind, I am not doing that," "Why not, they need to know their Grandmother," "They will, but I need you to step up as their Dad, and watch them," "Here we go again, I will be over there in a hour to see them," "Dude, whatever, if you have to say it like that then you don't need to see them," "Say it like what?" I asked, and Yvonne hung up the phone in

## WHAT IT TAKES TO BE THE MAN

my ear. What in the hell is wrong with that woman? Why must black men go through shit like that with their children's Mother, I thought.

Yvonne made me have high blood pressure. I sat behind my computer and at my house, "How did this woman get so mean? Why is she like this? I believe she needs a doctor for a mental health examination.

I hated that she was taking my children to her sister's house. There are thugs and gangsters are down the streets selling drugs and who knows what. I got showered and dressed, and I left the house early in the morning, hoping to talk her out of taking my children over to her sisters and dropping them at Momma's house.

Soon, as I pulled up to Yvonne's house to see my children, she pulled out of her driveway and put them in the car. "Where are you going?" "I have to go somewhere; you said you would be here around 4 pm," "And you said you have to be at work at 4 pm, or you were dropping them off at your sister's house,"

For a moment, Yvonne got quiet because my children were calling out to me. "Hey, Dad, I love you," my son said. I love you, Daddy," my daughter said. At that moment, I was so delighted.

"Okay, here, take them. I have things to do before I go to work. The next time, tell me you are coming. Don't be coming over here unannounced," Yvonne said maliciously.

# WHAT IT TAKES TO BE THE MAN

A part of me wanted to say something nasty back to her, but I couldn't because my children were so happy to see me, and I was glad to see them.

I ignored Yvonne's intelligent comments and told my children to get into my car. I drove off fast. It's annoying how she acts; she doesn't even care if it affects our children. On top of that, she has three other children with two different baby daddies.

I still remember when she said I would have children by other women when we separated, but instead, it's her with all those damn baby daddies. I hated how she made me feel less than a man, but sometimes life has a way of humbling people and one day, Yvonne will get what's coming to her.

My children and I went to the park. All these negative thoughts about their Mother went away as we made each other laugh. They were my joy, and the more I watched them play together, the more it made me want to be a better man. The love that they showered upon one another was a joy to see.

After we finished in the park, I took them to get ice cream. While eating ice cream, I listened to them tell all these bad stories about their Mom and her boyfriends. I was worried that my children would end up being mentally disturbed after listening to all those crazy tales. I knew then that I shouldn't give up on my dreams because I wanted my children away from that crazy environment. After enjoying my children, it was time to take them to their Mom. They didn't want to return them and wanted to stay with me so badly. I told them it was out of my control, but I would come over to their aunt's house for a while if they wished to. That made them very happy and excited.

When I pulled up, Yvonne's car was in the driveway. She opened the door, and my son and daughter approached the house. They turned and said," I love you, Dad." That melted my heart. "I love you too," I said as I pulled off. I could see Yvonne rolling her eyes as I turned the corner of her street. I believe she needs to seek a psychologist.

My thoughts were interrupted when I received a phone call from Matthew Granite. "Hello, Mr. Bell. How are you doing?"

"I am doing fine, and yourself?" "I am doing well; I was just letting you know that I had a change of plans, and I am in your city today," "You are here; why? I thought you were coming in two weeks; what happened?" "Oh, nothing, things change; I have some business that I need to take care of, and it can't wait," "Does it have anything to do with my project?" "What?" "Your business. Is that why you are here?" "Not so much, but I do need to go to New York City in two days to follow up on a lead or two,"

"Oh, okay, I thought you already have leads." "I do; I plan on taking care for everything while here." "I am taking care of business two weeks ahead of time. I wonder what brought that on? "As I said, business just got pushed up. Hopefully, we can get together and have coffee and talk more about your plans when you sell your movie script," "Let me know now, and I am glad you are here," "Same here, Mr. Bell; I will be in touch with you," Matthew said.

I was confused about why he came early, but that was his business. I decided to call Amekia to see how she was doing, but she didn't answer.

Every time I called, her phone was forwarded to her answering machine. At that point, I figured she knew it was me calling. Why does she keep forwarding me to the answering machine? I said aloud. I only wanted to check on her, so I called again, and her phone was off this time. That worried me, and I didn't know if she was all right.

I was just about to go home when something told me to go to Amelia's house to see if she was okay. As far as I knew, she still had the flu. On my long drive there, I couldn't help but question Mr. Granite's sudden trip to Rochester. It made me wonder about his reason for just showing up, especially when he said he would be in town in a few weeks and still had no leads to sell my movie script.

My Momma called me as I was getting close to the exit on my way to Amelia's house. "Hello, Momma, what's going on?" "I just called you to tell you they still have not found Harold or his body," "That's not good, but I think someone may have killed him and buried his body," I said. "I don't think he would've stayed away from Vanessa this long," "I agree, Momma. Did Ella show up?" "Yes, that

## WHAT IT TAKES TO BE THE MAN

tramp did," "Where is she?" "Ella is at your grandmother's house with her children where she needs to be," "How is she?" "She is still crazy as hell," "Ha, ha, that's crazy, have you talked to Dad?" "Yes, he's over here, and he's trying to have sex with me," "What, he's what?" "You know, he's trying to get some," She chuckled. "Momma," "What, DeVon?" "I don't want to hear that," "You asked, and I told you, where are you? Are you coming by?" "I am out and about, not tonight." "I am surprised you are not behind that computer writing. Are there any leads yet?" "I was earlier, but I am working on some leads," "Don't worry, DeVon, your time is coming, just don't give up," I won't, thank you, Momma, I will talk to you later," "Okay, I will talk to you soon, bye, son," Momma said. I finally made it to Amelia's house, and as I pulled up, I could see a car in her driveway. The license plates on the vehicle were out-of-town plates. The car seemed to be a rental. I sat in front of her house and called her every time the phone went to the answering machine. For some reason, she kept forwarding my calls. Since I got no answers, I walked up to her door and rang the doorbell. I waited about ten minutes in front of her house while ringing the doorbell and calling her. I noticed the door was slightly open, but I didn't see anyone, so I went and sat in my car, and I waited and waited until I fell asleep. I awoke, and the car was still in her driveway. I backed my car down the street until the sun started rising. I couldn't believe I was outside Amelia's house waiting like some jealous boyfriend, but I was doing that.

## WHAT IT TAKES TO BE THE MAN

Suddenly, I could see someone who looked like a man coming out of her front door. I started my car, and I drove by slowly. I looked up at the guy and Amelia, who stood in the doorway with a short robe on while smiling. The guy lifted his head as I reached the front of her house. I was pissed off to see it was Matthew Granite coming out of Amelia's house.

Amelia saw my car, and she immediately slammed the front door. I know she thought I didn't see her, but I did. I wanted to get out and kick Mr. Granite's ass so much, but I realized that would lead me to jail. I drove away from there, and I cried all the way home. A few times, I turned around and wanted to confront her, but I knew the consequences would be too significant.

I made it home, and I started shooting shit around. I couldn't believe I had been betrayed like that. All this time, I gave Amelia the benefit of the doubt. My Momma was right, and I was in denial. How could I let my guard down? I felt like a loser; I felt like half a man. Why would she sleep with this older man? I kept racking my brains on why she would do that, but there was no reasonable explanation. Point blank, Amelia was disloyal and a liar. I knew that now. That night, I didn't get any sleep. By morning, Mr. Granite left an email that said, "I am not going to be able to represent you; I couldn't find any buyers; maybe you should try and get in touch with another agency,"

## WHAT IT TAKES TO BE THE MAN

I looked at his email with a smirk, and I emailed back, "Fuck you and your services," I blocked him and even on my phone. I never wanted to speak to him again. The more I thought about how funny Amelia acted as of the late, the more I saw why.

She thinks sleeping her way to the top will work for her. That's her business. Amelia won't ever have to worry about me again. I felt ashamed, but I immediately picked myself up. I realized this was another distraction that I must conquer.

I didn't want to tell my Momma she was right, so I didn't say anything to her that day. As the day went on, though, my heart was broken, and I couldn't believe it, so I drove back out to Amelia's house that night to make sure I saw what I saw, and this time it was worse. I walked up to her window and saw the two of them kissing. I slowly moved away from her window and ran to my car. Why did I do that to myself? It only made me hurt more.

I heard her door open, so I ducked into the bushes. Amelia looked out one way, and Mr. Granite looked out the door in the other direction. I could hear them laughing and giggling when they finally returned to the house. It was funny to them, but to me, I had never felt pain like this. I trusted her, and she betrayed me. It always seems like the people you care about most will cross you. I knew I had to move on, but how?

# Chapter 26

## *From Defeat To Triumph*

I was so irate as I drove home; I started pounding my steering wheel while asking myself, "How dumb, how dumb am I?" I should never have introduced the two of them. I thought I was doing the right thing, but I was a fool. I made it home, and I put myself down all night. I wanted to call Amelia and curse her out, but my pride wouldn't let me stoop that low. Tears rolled down my cheeks because deep down inside, I wanted to hurt Mr. Granite, too. I realized that they weren't worth it. I finally fell asleep with a massive headache.

By morning, I felt even worse. Things changed when I received a phone call from Mr. Trevor Belchem from a substantial literary agency in New York City. Somehow, he heard about me through someone at one of the Film Festivals I attended.

## WHAT IT TAKES TO BE THE MAN

I emailed him a copy of my transcripts, and he immediately said he wanted to meet with me as soon as possible. I was so happy because he kept praising the transcript. Mr. Belchem and I chatted for hours.

The conversation was going so well that we started discussing everything else. After we finished, we scheduled a date to meet as soon as I could make the trip to the Big City.

I was glad he called because it took my mind off killing Amelia and Mr. Granite. Now, I had something to look forward to. My dreams were about to come to the forefront. Amelia will be sorry that she betrayed me that way, I told myself.

Mr. Belchem said he would pay for my airfare and hotel stay. That's when I knew this was real. Things sounded too good to be accurate, but Mr. Belchem said he already had some leads in mind for my movie script to be sold, which lifted my spirits. That made me so elated. Now, what could keep me down? I thought after I hung up the phone.

I was so excited I ran out of the house to tell my Momma the good news in person. As I turned the corner from my street, my phone started ringing. At first, I ignored it, and it rang again. I began to turn off the ringer, but it rang so much< that I decided to answer it finally.

## WHAT IT TAKES TO BE THE MAN

I heard yelling and screaming just as I was about to say hello. "Who is this? What's going on?" "DeVon, please come to the hospital," Yvonne's sister screamed. "To the hospital, why, what's going on?" I yelled. "DeVon, please come to the hospital; your son has been shot," Yvonne's voice screeched.

"What the fuck happened, I yelled at the top of my lungs. "Stop cursing; this is serious; your son has been shot. I am unsure if it's serious," Yvonne said. "I told you I didn't want my children over there," I yelled. "Will you two stop arguing, DeVon, get your ass here now," Yvonne's sister said loudly.

"I am coming; I am coming. How is he?" I yelled. "I am not sure, but I think the doctor said he hopes it's a flesh wound," "A flesh wound, was he still conscious?" I asked. "He was at first, but as soon as the ambulance came, he fainted; DeVon, come, come, now, I can't lose my son," Yvonne screamed. : What hospital?" I yelled. "We are at Northside General Hospital; hurry," She said while crying. I hung up the phone; I called Momma and Dad and told them to meet me at the hospital. I could hear my Momma screaming at the top of her lungs, and Dad was trying to calm her down as I hung up the phone.

I was crying and in shock at the same time. I started praying to God as I got closer to the hospital. Who would shoot my ten-year-old son? He didn't deserve this, I yelled aloud. I reflected on how I told Yvonne not to let my children go to her sister's house. That area is full of people who want to be gangsters. I know because I was once in the shoes of a street gangster. "I don't deserve this," I yelled as I pulled into the hospital parking garage. I jumped out of my car and ran into the emergency entrance. The first person I saw was Yvonne crying and hugging her sister.

"What happened? How is he? Where is he?" I questioned them.

"The doctors are checking him," Yvonne's sister said as she held Yovonne.

"What's going on? How did this happen? Who did it?" I asked.

"The bullet wasn't meant for him; it was these crazy fools that live a few houses down from me; their house got shot up from a drive-by," Yvonne's sister said.

"My son, my son, our son," Yvonne yelled, crying. I felt so bad, and I started crying. "I am sorry, I am sorry, I didn't listen to you," Yvonne said as she walked over and hugged me. I hugged her back because, besides our differences, we had children together, and I felt her pain. "Where are the damn doctors?" I asked. "They said they would be coming out," Yvonne's sister said. "Yes, but that was almost an hour ago," Yvonne said. Momma and Dad came running into the hospitals and asked me all these questions. I was about to answer, but the doctor came out.

## WHAT IT TAKES TO BE THE MAN

"What's going on, doctor? How is he?" We all asked. "There is some good news: the bullet grazed your son; it is a flash wound; he will be okay," Doctor Heath said calmly.

"Good, good, oh my son," Yvonne said as she wiped her tears. "That's good to hear, doctor," Momma said, and Dad sighed.

"I am glad my nephew is all right," Yvonne's sister said as she walked away.

"Did they catch the person that shot him?" Momma asked Yvonne. "I heard they knew who did this; I have to call them," Yvonne said. "I hope they are caught and go straight to jail," Dad added.

"Why did he pass out if it's only a flesh wound?" Yvonne asked the doctor. "He went into shock. It's normal; the little flesh would heal in a few days. Let me go back here and check on him and do some paperwork, but the good thing is he will be okay, okay, bye," Dr. Heath said. I was so happy to hear the news about my son. Yvonne kept apologizing to me while crying.

"Stop crying, and call the police to see if they caught whoever did this?" I said. Yvonne's sister walked back into the lobby with her hand on her chin as if she were in deep thought. I didn't say one word to her because I was too pissed off. After hours, the doctor let us into the room to see my son, and he was gaining consciousness. We all hugged her and told him we loved him. Going through this with my son was a very humbling experience. That phone call was something that no black parent ever wanted to get. I was so blessed that God spared my son's life.

The next day, the hospital released my son. I stayed with him the entire day while over at Yvonne's house. I kept talking to him and praying over him. Yvonne's phone rang after I prayed over him, and she hurried up and answered it.

"Hello, yes, this is her, what, say what, you caught the guys who did the drive by, oh my God, yes, please, keep in touch, I hope he rots in jail for shooting a ten-year-old boy, he could've killed my son, okay, yeah, bye," Yvonne said. "They caught him?" I asked. "Yes, I can't wait to see his face, and if I get a chance, I will spit in his face," Yvonne said angrily. "Do you want to go to jail?" I asked. "I don't care; he could've killed my baby," She said. "I understand that you don't think I want to kill him too?" Yvonne started crying hard. "I am sorry, I'm sorry, I get it, but we have to do what's right for our son," "You're right, I have to calm down," "Don't get me wrong, the shooter deserves anything that he gets, the old me would have just handled it myself, but I must stay out here to protect my children, I can't protect them in jail if I go and do something stupid like take this into my own hands," I said. "You are right," Yvonne said as she hugged me. I looked at her hesitantly, and I held her as she cried. "We have to stop crying; we are waking him up," I said, and my son started moving

# WHAT IT TAKES TO BE THE MAN

around in the bed. As it got late, I finally headed home. I called Momma and Dad, and I then filled in everything that was going on. My son was lucky to be alive, and we were fortunate to have him amongst the living still. A few days later, the shooter was arrested. Knowing that he would be brought to justice lifted my spirits. Growing up as a black man, we have so many obstacles that intersect our paths. It's not only us parents; it's the love and prayers that our children don't fall victim to a world that is sometimes unfair to African Americans. I prayed that my load would get more manageable, and just as I finished my prayer, my phone rang. "Hello, Mr. Bell, this is Mr. Belchem. How are you doing, Sir?" "Not too good, but I am making it the best way that I can," "Well, I hope my news will make you feel a little better," "What news is that?" I asked. "I would like you to come to New York City in a couple of days, and I talked to a film producer who loved your transcripts; I just let him read a little; as we speak, I am working on your query letter and your package for him to look over, I am pretty confident that he will want to buy your movie script,"

"Are you for real?" I said excitedly," "Yes, I am serious. He loved your work and would like to meet you this Friday. Can you make it? Remember, I have your fare to get here," "Yes, yes, I will be there, just give me the time and place," "I will email you everything you need to know, from your hotel to your ticket for your flight, I am excited to work with you," Mr. Belchem said with enthusiasm.

## WHAT IT TAKES TO BE THE MAN

"Let me get everything situated, and I will wait for your email," "Okay, and one other thing: you said you have a few movie scripts, correct?" "Yes, one I do. I had it on a flash drive, but it disappeared, but I happen to have it copied and copy written too," "That's excellent; if you don't mind, send that movie script also," "I can't believe this; are you serious?" "Yes, I am. Your big break is here, and this could be what you've been waiting for; make sure you bring a nice suit, and we will talk together. I will make sure you get a good lawyer, and we will get this ball going," "All right, I will send the movie script as soon as I get off the phone," "Okay, make you look out for an email from me," Mr. Belchem said as we hung up.

I sent off the email, received Mr. Belchem's email, and dropped to my knees. The tears started flowing, and I started praying to God. I couldn't believe this was happening, but at the same time, I was crying because I realized that God kept my son alive. I was so blessed that he didn't die because if he had, I don't know if I would have made it in this world. Parents shouldn't be burying their children, and when that happens, it messes up legacies and the laws of nature.

I had to tell Momma the good news, so I headed to her house. On the way there, I called Dad, who was at Momma's house. I wonder why they don't get back together. They are both at a place where just being friends is okay. I wish I could reach that maturity, but I don't think Yvonne is there.

## WHAT IT TAKES TO BE THE MAN

I walked into Momma's house with one of the biggest smiles. "What are you smiling about, did they catch the guy who shot my grandson?" Momma asked. My smile slowly fell off my face. "Yes, they caught him, and I hope he does life in prison," I said. "And I wish I could kill him myself," Momma yelled. "He will get his, don't you worry; somebody is going deep to do more than that, like, get his butt hole, you know how they do in prison," Dad said. "I don't know about that, but he will get some time," I said. "A long time," Dad said. "I can't believe you are talking about somebody getting someone's butt hole, you are nasty," Momma said to Dad.

Dad sat there with a stupid look on his face. "Don't say anything, Dad," I said. "He better not, talking about somebody's butt hole," Momma laughed, and so did we. "You know what I mean," Dad said with a smirk. "You two are unconventional," I laughed. Momma ignored me and rolled her eyes.

"DeVon, what's the good news?" Momma and Dad asked. I told them about my trip and about selling my mobile script to a literary agent in New York City, and they were so excited and proud of me because I didn't quit my journey.

"We hope you go out there and make it big; so many young black men get stuck in the hood, and they just accept it. I am glad you are following your dream, son," "Your Dad is right; you are on the right path, and don't let anything stop you; time after time, we see young black men kill one another, and if it isn't that, the police are killing us, you remember what you had to go through with the police," Momma said. "How could I forget," I said. "Life is hard, son, especially for black folks," Dad said. "You go, son, and make your family proud, make yourself proud, and most importantly, those beautiful children of yours," Momma said. I walked over to Momma and Dad, and I hugged each of them. We chatted a bit more, and then I left to head home.

I needed to tell Yvonne what was going on because I knew she would have a damn fit if I didn't tell her that I was going out of town and her son had just got out of the hospital after being shot and almost killed. No matter what, I know she will curse me because that's what she does. I took my time dialing her phone number and thought about what I would say and how she would react, so I tried to prepare myself for the worst.

"Hello, Yvonne, uhm, I have to go out of town to meet with this literary agent; I will only be gone for a few days,"

"I am sitting here with your son, but then do what you must do? I will be here taking care of him. Are you at least going to see him before you leave? He has been asking for you?" I was shocked at her response; she was nice. "Yes, of course, it is now okay because I will fly out late tomorrow night," "Sure, yes, come on over, we will be waiting for you," When I heard that response, I nearly lost my damn mind. I had to look at my phone again to ensure I was talking to

## WHAT IT TAKES TO BE THE MAN

Yvonne. I pulled over onto the side of the road, and I put on my flashers. I couldn't believe Yvonne didn't curse me out and call me all kinds of names as she had done in the past.

After deep breathing, I pulled off and headed over to see my son. When I got to the house, Yvonne opened the door and told me to come in. "He's in my room. You can go in there. I have to cook these children some food," She said. I went, and I sat with my son as he slept. I kissed his forehead, patted him on his back, and prayed. I was so lucky to have my son alive. After an hour of sitting beside him, Yvonne entered the room and asked me if I was hungry. "Yes, I am hungry," I said. You can have dinner with us if you want to," She said. I am not going to lie; a part of me wanted to say hell no, but Yvonne's attitude towards me seemed to be some olive branch.

"Come and eat, Daddy," My daughter Imani said from the other room. I got up, and I got my plate. I had my dinner as I sat next to my daughter. At all times, I kept my eyes on Yvonne and the food. I wanted to make sure she wasn't trying to poison me or something, but the food was good. After I was done, I hugged and kissed my daughter on the cheek. "Go in there and hug your son before you go," Yvonne said. "Where are you going, Daddy," Imani said. "I will be back; I love you," I said. "I love you too," Imani said as I headed into the room to hug my son. As I was heading out the door, I turned to say bye to Imani, and Yvonne waved her hand at me and said, "Good luck," "Good luck, Daddy," Imani said. "Girl, get in this house; you don't

## WHAT IT TAKES TO BE THE MAN

even know why you are saying good luck," Yvonne said with a smile as she closed the front door. Again, I was taken aback by how she treated me respectfully. Maybe my son being shot changed and humbled her, I thought as I headed home. When I got into my apartment, I immediately started packing. My heart started pumping harder, and butterflies fell in my stomach, but simultaneously, I was trying to keep calm and still mentally. 'My mind was running a thousand times a minute.

I thought about all that I had been through, from getting molested by my Aunt Ella, being in the street selling drugs, being beaten by the police, and everything concerning Yvonne and my children. I feel blessed to have made it this far. Sometimes, the load a black man has to carry is so heavy and unbearable, but only the strong can survive in this world. The key to our success is **"Us."** Never give up, and always stay ready because when your time shows itself, you have to take advantage of it. After reliving all those thoughts and memories, I kneeled, prayed, and finished packing. Before I knew it, it was morning, and I was off to the airport.

I made it to New York City safely. I got my room in the hotel after pulling up all the information off my phone. Mr. Belchem definitely took care of everything. I was so excited as I dressed to meet him and hopefully speak to a film producer who wanted to buy my movie script. I was nervous as hell as I entered the building; I was literally shaking in my boots. Once I made it to his office, the butterflies went away. I entered his office, and it was time for business.

"Hello, Mr. Bell, come on in, Sir; I am glad you made it safely," He said. "Hello, Mr. Belchem, it's a pleasure, sir," "You didn't have a hard time finding our building, did you?" "A little bit, but I've been to the city a few times. I just asked a couple of people who just looked at me like I was crazy, but an old lady pointed me in the right direction," "Well, that's good, come, have a seat; I have some good news and some bad news," When Mr. Belchem said that, my shoulders slumped, and I felt deflated. "Bad news?" I asked. "Well, not bad for you, but it may concern you," "What is it?" I asked. "Would you like to hear the good news first," Mr. Belchem chuckled. "Yes, give me the good news," "The good news is that the film producer's company wants to buy your movie script at a good price," "Say what, are you for real? This is unbelievable," I said aloud. "I know it's your dream becoming a reality," "Oh my God," I said as I shook my head. "You did it, Mr. Bell; they love your work. Now we have to work out all the legal work, and we can make you a pretty wealthy man," He said.

I was still in shock in real-time. I didn't know what to say as I stood motionless with my mouth wide open. "Are you okay, Mr. Bell?" "Yes, yes, I am just trying to let this sink in; wow, is this for real?" I questioned Mr. Bell again. "Yes, so get used to it, but how do you want the bad news?" "I guess so; I should be able to handle it now," "I thought so," Mr. Belchem chuckled. I looked up the movie script you sent me, and it showed that someone tried to get copyrights for it already, but you already had the rights," "Say what, who was it, and how could they get my movie script?" "Do you know anyone named Amelia Davenport?" He asked. I was shocked, "Yes, she's an ex-girlfriend." "Well, her name came up, and someone who tried to copyright your movie script was there. Anyway, you gave it to her?" "Hell no, she must have stolen it. Did they let it go through?" "No, they didn't. Do you know why she would be this evil?" "I am not sure," Now, I know she is the one who stole my flash drive because it was on there, I thought. "Mr. Belchem, can I sue her for that?" "Yes, you can; I was just about to tell you to get a lawyer," "I have one; I will call him when I get back to the hotel," "Good, now back to the good news, let's celebrate," Mr. Belchem said. "I am all in, thank you," "No, thank you, and I look forward to working with you for a long time; you are very gifted, Mr. Bell." "Thank you again," "Now let's go get a drink," Mr. Belchem smiled.

We went to a nice restaurant in downtown Manhattan. While we were drinking and eating, some of Mr. Belchem's friends in the film industry came and sat at our table, and we chatted and drank until I felt really nice. "I have to go to my hotel now; I am feeling these drinks," I said. "I will drop you off at your hotel," Mr. Belchem said. All his friends praised me and welcomed me into the world of film. We all got up at the same time to walk out. Mr. Belchem paid the bill, and we left. I was still in shock, but I knew now that my entire life would change, and finally, for the better. After taking care of all the business the next day, plus getting my lawyer involved, I hopped on the first plane back home. I told everybody the good news. Momma cried. "We won't have to worry about money anymore, Momma," tears fell down my eyes. "I knew you could do it, son, I knew it," Dad said. "I know Yvonne is going to love this; she's going to come after your money," Momma said. "Don't even worry about that, son; those are your children; you know the right thing to do," Dad said. "What happened to Amelia? Did you tell her yet?" Momma asked.

Finally, I broke down and told them what happened with Amelia, and Momma kept shaking her head from side to side. "I told you she wasn't for you; your Momma knows best." "How did you know Momma?" "She's a liar; a woman knows another woman," she said. Yes, she was right; I gave her the benefit of the doubt," Dad said.

I told them how she was the one who stole my flash drive, and Momma got even angrier. Dad and I had to calm her down. "You better sue that disloyal, greedy whore," Momma yelled out. "Did you tell your children yet?" Dad asked. "No, but they will know," I said. "What do you think Yvonne will say?" "I don't know; before I left, she was being nice to me," I said. "Well, I am proud of you, son; go do big things," Dad said. "We love you; I am so proud of you, DeVon; you are a great man, and don't anyone tell you differently," Momma said.

## WHAT IT TAKES TO BE THE MAN

I never felt this good before in my life. The journey was long, not my time but God's time. I just kept working, and I kept faith. The past should never define you, only remind you of who you used to be. This is a new and exciting chapter of my life, and I am now **Mr. Edwin Bell, the screenwriter!**

# THE END!!!

Also, never let your environment interfere with your purpose; a black man or woman has to work and live as hard as anyone in a world that we help build. It takes passion and sacrifice to achieve your goals. No matter how far they seem, you can always reach them if you don't give up.

*This story is based on actual events; the characters are other young boys who are going through obstacles like DeVon Edwin Bell. Pray and keep God first, and the sky is the limit...*

*The streets are undefeated, so get out while you can. Make something of yourself, and make your family proud...*

*By*

**CHARLES LEE ROBINSON JR.**

Made in United States
Orlando, FL
15 August 2025